Rising. . .with brigh
Stars. . .that work th

Sarah was so mixed up, so confused.

She didn't deny that she had wanted Ren to kiss her. But he made her blood boil. Whether it was with anger, frustration, impatience or passion. It didn't matter. Ren Taylor made her *feel* things she didn't want to feel.

There was a knock on her door and Sarah quickly crossed the room to open it.

Ren stood in the hallway and announced, 'I've cancelled the hire car.' His voice reverberated through her body, the words echoing in her head. 'I've decided to stay.'

One special month, four special authors. Some of the names you might recognise, like Jessica Matthews, whose book this month is also the beginning of a trilogy. Lucy Clark and Jenny Bryant offer their second books, while **Poppy's Passion** *introduces Helen Shelton.*

Rising Stars. . .catch them while you can!

Dear Reader

What a joy to be able to write to you and create a stronger bond between author and reader.

DELECTABLE DIAGNOSIS is my second Medical Romance published by Harlequin Mills & Boon and is set in Tasmania, Australia.

After many years of polishing my technique and style, I learned my first Medical Romance, A SURGEON'S CARE, had been accepted for publication. On the day I received the contract, I also discovered I was pregnant with our first child— a beautiful little girl.

Being able to write Medical Romance books as a full-time occupation has been a real blessing for me and I can now concentrate on writing more Medical Romances as well as raising my family from the comfort of our own home.

I hope you have as much enjoyment reading DELECTABLE DIAGNOSIS as I had writing it.

With warmest regards,

Lucy Clark

DELECTABLE
DIAGNOSIS

BY
LUCY CLARK

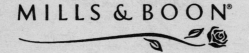

MILLS & BOON®

With many thanks to Virginia, the Sth. Aust. Romance Writers' Group,
Sue, Glenda and, of course, my husband—Peter. Proverbs 3:5-6

*First published in Great Britain 1997
Harlequin Mills & Boon Limited,
Eton House, 18-24 Paradise Road, Richmond, Surrey TW9 1SR*

© Lucy Clark 1997

ISBN 0 263 80377 5

*Set in Times 10 on 11½ pt. by
Rowland Phototypesetting Limited
Bury St Edmunds, Suffolk*

03-9709-47808-D

*Printed and bound in Great Britain
by Mackays of Chatham PLC, Chatham*

CHAPTER ONE

IT WAS a dark and stormy night.

The lightning cracked and the thunder roared. A high-pitched scream worked its way up from the depths of her lungs, escaping unheard from her lips as she tripped and fell to her knees.

Turning her head, she listened hard for the pounding of horses hooves along the sodden ground. It didn't matter how fast she could run. . .they would catch her in the end.

'Doc?' An urgent voice accompanied the pounding at the door. Sarah sprang out of her chair in fright, sending the book spiralling through the air.

'Doc, are you there?' The pounding persisted and Sarah mentally shook herself, before stalking to the door. This was definitely one of the drawbacks to being a country GP, she thought as she unlocked the bolt, disturbed at all hours of the day and night but Sarah loved her job.

'Yes, I'm here.' Sarah swung the door open and stood back to admit Mike, a seventeen-year-old who lived a few blocks away. She looked out into the night. It was dark and had been raining but no storms were on the horizon, at least not of the weather variety.

Mike moved aside as two men, carrying a third—obviously injured, from his blood-stained clothes—bustled their way up her front steps onto the verandah. Sarah glanced over at the clock on the mantel—quarter past ten.

'Where's the doctor?' one of the men barked after
he'd given her a brief glance. In normal circumstances
Sarah would have taken great umbrage at his tone but
her attention was fixed on the injured man.

'I'm the doctor,' she said firmly. 'Bring him through
to the theatre immediately.' She turned on her heel and
led the way along the hard wooden floors of the hallway
to the back of the house.

Holding open the door, she motioned the men to go
through into the theatre preparation area where there
was a barouche. Sarah noticed, as they passed her, that
their clothes were slightly torn.

'This is better than I'd hoped.' The man who had
spoken earlier stood with his hands on his hips after
they'd gingerly placed her patient on the barouche. He
peered through the small glass window positioned in
the centre of the heavy, metal theatre door.

He was well over six feet with short black hair that
was greying slightly at the temples and he spoke with
a strong British accent. His gaze locked with hers across
the small room and again he checked her from head
to toe.

Sarah defiantly stood her ground and when his eyes
finally returned to clash with the dark brown of her
own she levelled an insolent stare at him. 'If you've
quite finished, I'd like to attend to my patient. Mike,
contact Kate and tell her I need her, stat.'

'What about Ed?' Mike asked, his eyes wide with
alarm. Ed was a semi-retired anaesthetist who lived in
the community and was always willing to help Sarah.

'He's in Launceston this evening. Never mind,
we'll cope.'

Mike nodded and raced out of the room. She turned
and reached for the unconscious man's wrist. Auto-

matically counting the pulse, Sarah noted the result on a new patient information chart and reached for the sphygmomanometer.

'What's his name?' she asked.

'Steve Lewis.' The second man who had carried him in answered her question. He was considerably shorter than his friend and had a crop of auburn hair.

'Age. Marital status. Any allergies?' She checked Steve's pupils and noticed that he was coming round. She waited until his eyes were focused on her before saying in a softer tone, 'Hello, I'm Dr Rutherford.'

'What happened?' Steve asked, his voice weak and raspy.

'You fell down the cliff,' his auburn-haired friend told him then glanced at Sarah. 'We've been hiking since yesterday morning in the mountains. At approximately eight-thirty Steve abseiled down a cliff. His hand slipped off his rope and he fell down to the rock face below. Fortunately for him, he only had a few metres to go. I was half-way down and Ren. . .' he turned and pointed to his other friend, who was coolly surveying his surroundings '. . .was still at the top.

'By the time we got to Steve he was unconscious. We applied the tourniquets to stop the bleeding and carried him through the bush to your town. We went to the first house we came to and Mike led us to you.'

Steve had closed his eyes, his facial expression radiating the pain he was in. 'Is he allergic to any drugs?' Sarah asked as she scribbled down the information down.

'Not that I'm aware of.' He reached into the back pocket of his jeans and pulled out his wallet. He unfolded a piece of paper and handed it to Sarah. 'My name is Kevin Lefler and I'm an anaesthetist. We're all doctors.' He indicated his friends. Sarah read his medical registration certificate and gave it back.

The man Kevin had called Ren let out an impatient sigh. 'When you've quite finished, Dr Rutherford, perhaps we could proceed with Steve's operation? I assume you have a nurse tucked away in this little town?'

Sarah turned and gave him a brisk nod. 'Kate should be here soon.'

'Good, because Steve's complicated fractures of his tibia and fibula won't wait all night. Those arteries need clamping. Kevin, insert an IVT and get his pain stabilised,' he barked. 'We'll be operating within the hour, Dr Rutherford, so I suggest you get things ready.'

Sarah glared at him. 'I presume you have your registration certificate here, Dr. . .'

'No, I don't. My identification was lost on the way here. Kevin and Steve will have to vouch for me.'

'He's a qualified orthopaedic surgeon, Dr Rutherford,' Kevin said quickly. 'The best in the business. Steve couldn't have been more fortunate than to have the prof—'

'Just get on with it, Lefler,' Ren snapped, and Kevin grinned at Sarah.

'Don't mind him, he's always this rude. You'll get used to it.'

'I hope not,' Sarah mumbled under her breath as she helped Kevin to find the equipment he needed. Ren stayed with Steve and monitored him, while Sarah began getting the instruments ready.

Kate walked into the room and stood with her hands on her hips. 'This had better be worth it, Sarah. I don't like having my evenings disturbed. . . I've told you that before.'

Sarah ignored the middle-aged woman's retort and

turned to introduce the men. 'Kate, this is Dr Lefler, who will be anaesthetising, and Dr. . .' She gestured to Ren who still hadn't given her his surname and waited for him to supply it.

'Taylor,' he informed her as though he were talking to an insolent child. 'Dr Taylor.'

'Dr Taylor is apparently an orthopaedic surgeon who will be performing tonight's surgery. Steve Lewis. . .' she indicated the patient '. . .has, according to Dr Taylor, complicated fractures, to his tibia and fibula. So, if you wouldn't mind getting things ready, the sooner we operate the sooner you can go back home.'

'Yeah, sure,' Kate grumbled and Sarah held her breath and counted to ten. Although Kate was a competent nurse, her dedication was seriously lacking.

Sarah quickly went into her consulting room to call Trevor Ross, her farm manager, who was the pilot of the estate's plane and informed him of the situation. 'Can you have Rudolf ready to carry two passengers and one patient to Hobart? We'll be going into Theatre in a few minutes but it will be a few hours yet before we can transfer the patient. It will all depend on his post-operative recovery.'

'Will do,' Trevor acknowledged, and Sarah replaced the receiver. She buried her head in her hands and let out a deep breath.

'Whenever you're ready, Dr Rutherford.' A deep, sardonic voice spoke from her doorway and Sarah raised her head. Ren stood there, his thumbs hooked into the pockets of his jeans. Slowly Sarah let her eyes travel the length of his body. Hiking boots on his feet, an old pair of jeans that fitted him like a second skin and a warm shirt with sleeves rolled up to the elbows accentuated, rather than detracted from, his fine, muscled torso.

How could a man *that* great-looking be such a dictator? Sarah gave herself a shake. How could she think such sultry things about a man she didn't know?

'Are you ready *now*, Dr Rutherford?' he asked with an insolent stare when her eyes finally clashed with the blue of his. Sarah coloured at her open appraisal of him but lifted her head in defiance.

'Yes.' She stood and followed him back to the theatre.

'I'm assuming that "Rudolf" is an aeroplane and not the famous reindeer?' he said as they approached the scrub sink. He ripped off his shirt and bent to scrub his arms. Sarah felt her jaw drop open as her eyes were given the opportunity to appraise him further. Not a single part of his torso wasn't firm and well toned. He turned his head to look at her and she remembered that he'd asked her a question. Rudolf! He'd asked about the plane, she recalled quickly.

'Ah-h-h. . .that's correct,' she replied and forced her attention from him. Why did this complete stranger seem to attract her? Unable to supply the answer, she concentrated on scrubbing.

'Quite an asset to a small hick town like this.'

Sarah's emotions changed abruptly to annoyance at his comment. She took a deep breath and slowly exhaled. Kate reluctantly came over to assist in the scrubbing and gowning process. Between Kate's apathy and Ren's arrogant attitude Sarah hoped that this evening would pass with more speed. Steve was their first priority and how this forceful barbarian treated any of them was of no consequence at this moment.

'Once we've stopped any internal bleeding we'll take X-rays to determine the exact location of the fractures,' he continued in a commanding tone.

Kevin announced that Steve was anaesthetised and Sarah pushed personal feelings aside—they were all professionals and had a job to do. After they'd been working methodically for ten minutes Sarah quickly realised that Ren whoever-he-was was indeed an efficient surgeon. She gracefully bowed to his expertise and followed his instructions implicitly.

'I must say, Dr Rutherford,' he spoke quietly as he sutured an offending artery, 'that I am impressed by your little theatre. It has up-to-date equipment, portable X-ray facilities and even the fact that you had ortho-paedic plates and screws available for me to use is highly commendable. Suction, please.'

Sarah concentrated on her work rather than how much his compliments had pleased her. Ridiculous really. From what she'd seen of Ren so far he was domineering, dictatorial, overbearing and last, but not least, extremely arrogant. The fact that he seemed to be a competent surgeon didn't in any way cancel out those other 'qualities'.

If she kept her temper in check for just a few more hours he and his friends would be on their way back to Hobart, and she'd never have to see any of them again. Because if there was one specific type of male that Sarah didn't like it was one like Ren.

'We'll take a check X-ray to see if we've got it all, then suture him up.'

Kate X-rayed the patient and they all waited in silence for the films to be processed. Once they were ready the nurse hooked them onto the viewing box and Ren and Sarah walked over for a closer look.

'Looks fine,' Ren said, after peering at the films. 'Well done, Dr Rutherford.' His tone was still bland and Sarah wondered if he spoke to all of his staff this way. She could picture them—nurses, registrars and interns falling at his feet on hearing his heartfelt, lavish praise and thanking him immensely for actually noticing them and taking time to comment.

She shook her head and turned back to Steve. Someone ought to teach Ren the meaning of sincerity and *soon*.

They completed the operation without further complication or social communication. Once the anaesthetic had been reversed and they'd noted his state of consciousness they transferred Steve back to the barouche, degowned and wheeled him back to the preparation room.

'When will that plane be ready?' Ren asked as he shrugged back into his shirt.

Sarah glanced at the clock on the wall—two minutes to midnight. She rubbed her forehead, then let her fingers massage the back of her neck. 'When the patient's ready to be transferred,' she answered, unable to keep the sarcasm from her voice. She let her eyes flick over him and decided that she needed a serious jolt of caffeine to control her temper. She left Kevin and Kate monitoring the patient and walked into the hallway.

She had thought that Ren would follow her, but when there was no answer to her sarcasm she stopped short and turned. He was behind her all right. So close that he walked into her.

Sarah's hands reached out to stop herself from stumbling into him but it was too late. His arms settled around her waist and held her steady. With her hands on his chest and his arms enveloping her, anyone would have thought that they were embracing like two lovers.

Feeling her face flush with embarrassment, Sarah

looked up into Ren's face. He rewarded her with a mocking grin and dark, bushy eyebrows raised in amusement.

'Really, Dr Rutherford,' he drawled sardonically. 'If you wanted a cuddle you only had to ask.'

Sarah grunted in disgust and took a firm step out of his arms. She ignored the way her body had sprung to life at his touch. The way her fingertips had tingled with anticipation as they'd caressed his chest through the coarseness of his shirt. The way her sense of smell had delighted in his masculine scent. None of this was important.

Entering the kitchen, Sarah disregarded his deep chuckle and walked over to her coffee-pot. Automatically going through the motions, she tried to ignore the man behind her but her body seemed too aware of him, especially as she was still warm from his touch.

'How'd everything go?' Trevor asked as he casually walked into the kitchen and introduced himself to Ren, giving him a hearty handshake.

'Fine,' Sarah answered.

He nodded at her reply. 'Mike and I have collected your gear and stowed it in Rudolf.' He eased himself into a chair and offered one to Ren. Trevor was a typical farmer—a real country fellow—and Sarah, who had known him and his wife, Edith, since she was born, loved them both dearly. None of life's ups and downs seemed to faze either of them and they continued to view the world in their laid-back country way.

'So, you're all doctors, eh? Bit of luck that.' He glanced quickly at Sarah and nodded apologetically. 'Not saying that you can't handle things, missy,' he grinned, knowing that his nickname for Sarah would soften his words, 'but I'll tell you, Ren. In the twelve

months Sarah's been our doc she's had me playing a
porter, a nurse and helping in any other way she can
think of. Brilliant, she is. Pure brilliance. Her old man
would be as proud as punch, God rest his soul.'

Sarah wished he wouldn't ramble on in such a way,
especially to Ren. She didn't want him to know anything
about her. He was a complete stranger who had caused
her to feel a multitude of emotions, most of them annoying, in a few short hours and she looked forward to his
departure.

'That coffee almost ready, missy?' Trevor asked, and
stood to collect the milk from the refrigerator and the
sugar container from the shelf. 'No need to worry about
feeding your guests.' He patted Sarah's hand. 'Edith's
been making her famous country sandwiches and should
be here any moment.' He glanced down at his wrist-
watch as though expecting her to walk through the
door—which she did.

The look that passed between the couple made Sarah
feel all gooey and happy inside. They had been married
for almost thirty years and still their love radiated
around them.

'Where is everyone?' she asked, and deposited a huge
tray of sandwiches onto Sarah's kitchen table.

'Monitoring the patient. I was just about to take them
in a cuppa and relieve Kevin of his watch so he can
have something to eat.' Sarah poured a few cups and
placed the pot on the table. She watched as Ren picked
up a sandwich and began to eat heartily. Suddenly he
turned and caught her watching him. He stood as he
finished his mouthful and walked over to her.

'I need to contact the Royal Hobart Hospital to let
them know what's happened. May I use your phone?'

'Certainly. Use the extension in the consulting room,

or if you'd rather fax them please do so.'

'A fax as well.' Ren raised an eyebrow. 'More impressive gadgets, Dr Rutherford?' He didn't give her time to reply as he turned on his heel and left.

Edith bustled over to Sarah and gave her a hug. 'Hear you've been burning the midnight oil again.'

'You could say that,' Sarah replied with a weary smile and ran her fingers through her short blonde hair. 'I'm glad that tomorrow—' She stopped and corrected herself. 'I mean *today* is Sunday and I don't have a consulting clinic. I'm going to sleep for at least twelve hours straight, then go for a ride on Sebastian.'

Edith chuckled. 'It sounds like a wonderful plan, dear, but Lizzie Dumar's so close to having her baby I'm willing to bet today will be the day.'

Sarah sighed. Edith was usually right about these things.

'Do you want some food, love?' Edith asked and Sarah shook her head.

'No, thanks. I've got to help Kate clean the instruments and the theatre but first I'll give Kevin a breather.' She put the cups on a tray and carried them through to the preparation area. Kate was eager to sit and rest for a while and reached for the coffee. Sarah took a sip of hers, before going in to see how Steve was doing.

'There's coffee on that tray and food in the kitchen if you're hungry,' she told Kevin. 'I'll monitor Steve while you replenish yourself.' Sarah smiled at him and he grinned back.

'Thanks, Sarah. You're a champ.' He handed her the chart, before disappearing.

'Any food for me?' Steve whispered.

'Sorry, my friend. None for you at this time.'

Kevin returned and resumed his post-operative care, leaving Sarah free to get the theatre in order. Kate performed her duties reluctantly and the relief that could be read in her face when Sarah told her to go home was almost laughable.

'That's what I like to see—real dedication,' Ren's voice said from behind her, and Sarah spun around to face him. 'Why do up put up with her attitude, Dr Rutherford?'

'Because she's the only nurse in the community. She moved into the area about six months ago with her husband who's a farmer. As the community had been in desperate need of a nurse they offered her a position. Kate soon made it clear that she wasn't here to nurse and would only concede to help in emergency cases.' Sarah shrugged. 'So I have to put up and make do. Did you manage to get through to the hospital?'

'Yes. Thank you.' He added the last two words as though they were an afterthought. She could feel his gaze on her as she resumed her work. The sooner she got this theatre cleaned the sooner she'd be able to go to sleep, which was what her body was craving at the moment.

After a few more minutes of his silent appraisal Sarah let out an exasperated sigh and glared at him. 'Don't you have anything better to do?'

'No.' He remained where he was, leaning against the wall, arms crossed across his chest.

'Would you mind writing up the operation notes?'

'Finished, and I've even used your photocopier to take a copy for the hospital notes.'

'In that case, would you please go away so I can finish in peace?' Sarah had meant to be polite but her voice cracked on her last words, and for a horrified moment she thought she might break down in tears right in front of him.

'As you wish.' He inclined his head toward her and walked away.

The sooner they all left the better. She resumed her duties, scrubbing the theatre with more enthusiasm than was required.

It was another couple of hours before Steve was stable enough to be transferred to Hobart, and because both Ren and Kevin were doctors there was no need for Sarah to accompany the patient.

Edith had insisted on staying and helping out where she could, mainly making sure that everyone was adequately fed. It was after three o'clock that Sunday morning before Steve was carried out on the aeroplane's stretcher and put in the back of Trevor's car, ready for his journey to the airstrip. Ren nodded his head and bade her a polite goodbye while Kevin shook her hand vigorously and gave her a friendly slap on the back before climbing into the car.

'Whew!' Sarah wiped imaginary sweat from her brow. 'Am I glad this night is at an end.'

'Off you go to bed, love. I'll shut the house up on my way out.'

'Thanks, Edith. . .for all of your help. I know it's pointless to say that you shouldn't have gone to all of that trouble making the sandwiches—so I won't.'

'Good. At least you're learning.' Edith smiled and gave her a motherly hug. 'Now, bed!'

Sarah gladly did as she was told. Letting her body relax into the mattress, she sighed and reflected on her day. Unbidden into her mind came the memory of Ren. Handsome he might be but his dominant attitude had her body tensing in remembrance.

Forcing her mind to pick another topic, she chose her horse, Sebastian. Taking him for a long ride through the countryside always helped her unwind. If she weren't so tired now she would take him out for a gallop. Sarah yawned before turning over. Sleep claimed her instantly.

At the sudden loud noise Sarah flung out a hand and punched her alarm clock.

She groaned, realising that she'd set the alarm last night. Nine o'clock. . .and she was now wide awake.

Compelling herself to sit up, she stretched languorously before she climbed out of bed. Not bothering to put a robe over the thigh-length T-shirt she wore, she padded to the bathroom. Only eight weeks till Christmas. Edith had invited her to spend Christmas with them, an offer she had gratefully accepted.

Sarah wandered sleepily into the kitchen and started the coffee. Making some toast, she reflected on the previous Christmas. Not only had it been extremely hectic patient-wise but her father had been critically ill and had died two days after the twenty-fifth. All burdens and grudges between them had been swept aside with a verbal profession of love from him, leaving her sorry that it hadn't happened sooner. In the few months before his death they had grown closer and talked more than during Sarah's entire thirty-two years.

'I'm sorry for treating you the way I did.' Sarah could easily recall his gravelly voice. 'But you're the spitting image of your mother. Every time I looked at you I resented the fact that you were here and she wasn't. I still miss her. It's a pity you were only a toddler when she died as you have no real memories of what a wonderful woman she was.' He'd sighed and looked off dreamily into the distance.

'The older you got the worse it became. Finally, I could take it no longer. That's why I sent you away to boarding school. I felt guilty about my feelings. I'm sorry, Sarah.' He'd gripped her hands and given her a watery smile. 'I didn't know what else to do.'

Sarah sipped her coffee, her eyes misting over with tears at the memories.

'Mmm, that coffee smells great.' A masculine drawl interrupted her thoughts. Sarah looked up, startled, to see a shirtless Ren, lounging in the doorway. He was stretching his arms upwards, an action which caused his denim jeans to lower slightly in front, giving her an overwhelming view of just how perfectly he was put together.

Sarah's coffee-cup slipped out of her hands and smashed on the wooden floor.

'Careful, Sarah.' He gave her a maddening grin. 'Just as well you were almost finished, otherwise you could have burnt yourself.' He sauntered toward her. 'Any left in the pot?'

Sarah, who had been leaning against the bench, quickly shifted out of his way and collected the dustpan and brush. If I were a cartoon, she thought, I'm sure he would see steam blowing out of my ears.

Feeling the fires of her temper blaze to life, Sarah rounded on him the minute she'd finished cleaning up the mess.

'That was my favourite cup,' she said between clenched teeth. 'What on earth are you doing in my house?' She glared daggers at him and hoped they'd hit their mark. 'Especially dressed like that!' she added, gesturing at his attire—or lack of it.

Ren remained silent for a moment and took up the position she'd vacated, leaning against the bench. 'What's wrong with the way I'm dressed? At least everything of mine that is considered indecent has been covered.' He sipped his coffee as his eyes travelled appreciatively over her long legs.

Feeling more self-conscious than ever before, Sarah crossed her arms defensively in front of her. 'Why are you still here? And how did you get in?'

'You know, Sarah.' He ignored her battle stance. 'Between the two of us we make up a whole outfit. I've got the lower half and you have *definitely* got the top. Just exactly how tall are you?'

'Five feet ten,' Sarah ground out. 'Now answer my questions.'

'All right,' he drawled in that sardonic, extremely British way. 'Don't have a hissy fit. Sit down and relax. Can I get you another cup of coffee?'

Sarah sat down but only because she was still feeling self-conscious under his appraising gaze and the table would provide a shield.

Ren carried two coffee-cups to the table and sat opposite her. 'You make good coffee.'

'The machine makes it. I just pour the water in. Now get on with it.' She was sick of him trying his macho charm on her and wished he'd stop ignoring the main question.

'Well, we were all in the plane when a flash of lightning erupted through the sky. A UFO appeared to be holding us in a stabilising beam. Suddenly a flash of light blinded me and the next thing I knew I was on their ship.

'They took me to their galaxy and put me through

a multitude of tests. They drained all my energy and
intellect. . .'

'Hoo-ray,' Sarah mumbled quietly to herself. If Ren
heard he ignored her.

'They brought me back to Earth and dumped me in
one of your far paddocks. First of all, I didn't know
where I was. Walking blindly through the night, I finally
came across your home. The back door was closed but
unlocked. Knowing that you wouldn't mind, under the
circumstances, I stumbled into your spare room and fell
asleep immediately.

'The most amazing thing is that the entire trip was
instantaneous.' He spread his hands wide. 'The next
thing I knew the smell of freshly brewed coffee was
wafting through the air, waking me from my near-death
experience.' He looked at her with a sorrowful
expression. 'Now, aren't you sorry you yelled at me?'

'Get out of my house.' Sarah said each word slowly
and precisely as she rose from the table. 'I no longer
care why you are here but I want you out. . .now.' At
that moment the telephone rang and Sarah walked over
to the bench and snatched up the receiver.

'You mean you don't believe me?' she heard him
ask incredulously.

'Dr Rutherford,' she snapped into the phone. 'It's
OK, John,' Sarah said after a pause. 'I was expecting
you to call. How far apart are the contractions?' She
waited for the answer, then said, 'Right. I'll be there
in twenty minutes. You're doing fine, and don't panic.'

After replacing the receiver, Sarah shook her head.
'Damn if that woman isn't right every time.'

'Who?' Ren asked. She had temporarily forgotten
that he was there, but only temporarily. She ignored
him for a little longer while she quickly rang Kate—

who was not so thrilled at being woken after such a long night—and informed her of the situation. She turned to face Ren.

'I have to deliver a baby. When I get back I want you gone. You let yourself in so you can let yourself out.' She turned and walked determinedly out of the kitchen and slammed her bedroom door shut with great relish.

'Does this mean you don't want me to help with the delivery?' she heard him call.

Flinging open her wardrobe, she grabbed at a pair of faded jeans and a shirt, seething inside at his audacity. If she could just punch him in the nose—once—she would feel much better!

CHAPTER TWO

'THAT'S it, Lizzie. One more push,' Sarah encouraged as she controlled the delivery of the baby's head. A few seconds later she said softly, 'OK, now I don't want you to push. Remember your breathing exercises, Lizzie.' Sarah slid her fingers around the baby's neck to check that the cord wasn't looped there. Thankfully, it wasn't.

'You're doing a wonderful job, Lizzie. Keep breathing—that's it.' She wiped away the mucus from the baby's mouth and nostrils, while waiting for the shoulders to rotate internally. She glanced up at Lizzie's husband, John, who had his back to Sarah and was doing his best to support his wife with her breathing techniques.

Sarah guided the shoulders out and the following contraction was sufficient to accomplish the expulsion of the body. The clock was checked and the time of birth noted. Kate held out the instruments for Sarah to clamp and cut the cord and a loud wail pierced the air, as though the little chap was telling them to put him back.

She quickly wiped him down then held him up so that Lizzie could see her beautiful son. John glanced over his shoulder, a tear in his eye.

'A son. . . Lizzie, we have a son!' He bent down and kissed his wife. Sarah placed a towel under the baby, before handing him to Lizzie.

'He's got a healthy set of lungs.' Sarah smiled as she

watched Lizzie gently take hold of her son's waving
fist and caress it.

'I'd like to do his evaluations now,' Kate said and
reached for the child.

Sarah frowned at Kate's brisk manner. Did nothing
stir this woman? Not even the miracle of life? Lizzie
looked as though she was ready to cry and Sarah quickly
intervened, keeping her tone light yet pointed. 'I think it
can wait for a few moments longer, Kate. He's breathing
well, his colour is good and it can be seen from here
that his arms and legs move well.'

Kate glared at Sarah but she ignored it. Lizzie gave
her son a kiss on his forehead and held him out for
Sarah to take, which she did with an encouraging smile.
'We'll have him back to you in a jiffy. You relax and
decide what you're going to call him.'

While Kate tended to the baby Sarah checked Lizzie's
pulse and blood pressure, before continuing with further
examinations. An injection of Syntometrine was given
to Lizzie to prevent postpartum haemorrhage, while
little Reuben—as he'd been named—was given an
injection of Vitamin K.

Once Kate had finished her observations she wrapped
him up and returned him to his proud mother for his
first feed. As Kate had had more experience than Sarah
with breast-feeding, she left them to it and began to
clean up the delivery area.

It was over three hours later that Sarah took her leave.
Kate would stay and monitor the patients. As she walked
out to her car Sarah's heart grew envious. She would
dearly love to have children one day. Her only problem
was finding Mr Right to have the babies with. She
smiled to herself as she envisaged Edith, fussing about
like an expectant grandmother. Although all her chil-

dren had 'left the nest' none had yet settled down and married.

She and Trevor had accepted Sarah into their hearts and treated her as another daughter. Almost two years ago they had agreed to manage her father's property when he'd fallen ill. Josiah Rutherford had been a proud man and when he'd finally asked Trevor and Edith, two long-time friends, to help him out they had left the farm they'd been managing in the Northern Territory and had taken up residence immediately.

Although, in the legal sense of the word, Sarah was their employer she certainly didn't feel that way. Trevor and Edith managed the farm with such diligence and devotion—as though it was their own. Sarah knew that without their support the farm would have had to be sold.

Knowing that Edith had predicted the arrival of Lizzie's baby, Sarah took a detour to their house. Bluey, her father's old farm dog, wandered over to greet her. He'd been living with the Rosses since her father had taken ill. Sarah dropped to her knees and gave him a scratch and a cuddle. He was getting on now and it looked as though arthritis might be afflicting his hind legs.

'Go and find Trevor,' she urged the dog with a pat. 'I've got to talk to Edith.' Bluey ambled off as his mistress had suggested, and Sarah walked over to the back door.

'Welcome, missy. Sit down and take the weight off your feet,' Edith said the moment Sarah appeared. 'Now tell me all about it. Did she have a boy or girl?'

'Your insight is amazing,' Sarah chuckled. 'A boy. A beautiful eight-and-a-half-pound boy. Reuben John they've called him, and Lizzie had no trouble delivering.'

Edith handed Sarah a handkerchief and pulled hers from her sleeve. 'Delightful.' They both dabbed their wet eyes before Edith said, 'I'll bet John didn't cut the cord. Always was a queasy lad. Did he at least stay with Lizzie?'

'Yes, he did but he had his back to me the entire time,' Sarah smiled. 'Some men can and some men can't.'

'I don't think I want to know what this conversation is about,' Trevor said as he came through the back door into the kitchen.

'It's nothing like what you're thinking,' Edith chuckled. 'Young Lizzie's had a baby boy and John's a bit queasy when it comes to things like that. Now, Sarah, you probably haven't eaten since breakfast, and Trevor and I were just about to have some afternoon tea. So you stay right where you are and we'll get you fed.'

Sarah knew that it would be futile to refuse. Edith always cooked enough for a small army and usually had plenty of left-overs. She also supplied two meals a day for Sarah, which could be found slowly simmering away in her oven or inside the microwave, waiting to be reheated.

Edith had told Sarah that her job was doctoring. 'The community needs a healthy doctor who's eating right and looking after herself,' she'd said to Sarah often enough. Edith had also insisted on cleaning Sarah's house once a week. At this Sarah had strongly protested, but Trevor had calmly informed her that it was useless.

'She sees you as one of her own, missy. Let her do it. It's her way of showing you how much she loves you.' His words had brought a lump to her throat, and for the past twelve months that was the way things had been done.

'Has Ren's hire car turned up yet?' Trevor asked.

Sarah choked on her mouthful, which resulted in Edith firmly pounding her back. 'You mean you know he's here?'

'Sure do. I was the one who gave him the key.' Trevor said matter-of-factly.

'Why?'

'Well, because the plane was cramped and he's still got a few more weeks of holidays left. So he decided to hire a car and see a bit more of Tasmania. Do you know he's been in Hobart for twelve months and this is the first break he's had from the hospital? How can anyone work that long without a break?'

'You and Edith do,' Sarah felt compelled to point out. 'And when you do go away it's because one of your children needs helping.'

Edith laughed. 'She's got you there, my love.'

'Yes, but I like what I do. I don't consider it work,' Trevor defended himself.

'Exactly!' Sarah smiled at him. 'That's exactly how I feel and probably how Ren feels too. But that doesn't explain what he was doing half-naked in my kitchen this morning, scaring the living daylights out of me.'

'Ooh, was he really?' Edith's eyes twinkled. 'What did he look like?'

'Edith!' Sarah reprimanded and Trevor chuckled.

'Don't get your knickers in a knot,' Trevor said. 'There was no room at the pub and it was nearly sunrise. The man was tired.'

'So why didn't he come back here?'

'Because Edith would have thought he was a burglar

and shot him. You, on the other hand, sleep like a log. Now stop fussing. The hire car has probably arrived and he'll have left long ago.'

'I hope so.' Sarah took a long sip of her drink.

'Pity you don't want him to stay,' Edith sighed as she cleared the plates away. 'I like him.'

'Oh, brother,' Sarah groaned. 'If that's your attitude I think I'll leave.' She stood and kissed Edith on the cheek. 'Thanks for the meal.' Sarah went back to her four-wheel-drive and drove along the dirt track to her home.

Going into the kitchen, she poured herself a cool drink. These November days were often hot one day and pouring with rain the next. The phone rang and as she was beside it she caught it on the first ring.

'Dr Rutherford.'

'Hi, this is Toni from TransHire. Is Ren there, please?'

Sarah frowned. 'No. I'm sorry, but he's already left.'

'Oh,' the husky female voice at the other end faltered. 'Well, he told me he'd be there until at least eight-thirty tonight. Could you leave a message for him?'

Sarah pulled the receiver away from her face and poked her tongue out at it. Who did they think she was—Ren's answering service?

'If you could just tell him that there's been a slight hitch in plans. The car we had lined up for him has been in an accident. We're trying to source another model exactly the same as his specifications, but we won't be able to have it there until tomorrow afternoon. Thank you very much and have a nice day.' Click. The line went dead.

Sarah replaced the receiver. At least Ren had told

the truth to Trevor about hiring a car. Oh, well, he could just stay at the pub tonight.

She decided that the first task on her administrative agenda was to quickly write up Lizzie's notes, before beginning the rest of her paperwork. Sarah opened the door to her consulting room and stopped dead. Ren stood by the examination couch and was tending a boy of about nine. Two adults were seated opposite them, watching intently everything he did.

Not wanting to undermine his authority in front of the patients, Sarah mumbled a quick 'Sorry,' before retreating. She stormed out to the stables and quickly saddled her horse. Riding Sebastian was always a good remedy for calming her ruffled feathers.

Almost two hours later she returned. Exhausted. Her anger and frustration at Ren obviously taking over her practice had diminished, although she was still going to demand an explanation.

Finding him seated comfortably in her lounge room with his feet up and reading a book, Sarah's annoyance returned.

'Why are you still here?' she said, her voice dangerously calm.

'I'm waiting on a hire car and then I'll be out of your hair.' He didn't bother to lower the book or even look at her.

'Well, your precious hire car won't be here until tomorrow. They called a few hours ago and left a message. Obviously you were too busy treating *my* patients to answer the call yourself.'

Ren slowly lowered the book and let his eyes assess her. 'Aren't you rather hot in jeans?'

Why did he do that? It didn't matter what she said he ignored her, trying to be cute and charming instead.

Well, it didn't work on her. She balled her hands into fists and tried again.

'Will you please tell me why you were in *my* consulting room, treating *my* patients, and then tell me why you haven't left *my* house.'

'Possessions are very important to you, aren't they, Sarah?'

Although she was tempted to storm over and slap his face Sarah tried to cool her temper, knowing that she wouldn't get any answers from him if she resorted to physical violence. 'Please answer my question,' she said through gritted teeth.

Ren stood. She noticed that he, also, was wearing jeans and wondered why he'd made that crack at her.

'First of all, they weren't your patients.'

'But this is *my* practice.'

'If you want your answer please don't interrupt. They are from Hobart and they were staying with friends. The children were watching the farm hands dehorn the calves. Well—' a smile lit his eyes '—one of the horns flew across and hit little Jimmy just above the eye. Problem was that the calf's blood then splattered over his face. Of course he covered his eye in agony and ran to the house.

'His mother managed to prise his hands away from his eye, only to reveal a mass of blood running down his face. Panicking, they rang here and I told them to bring him in.' He held his hands up in self-defence at the glare Sarah gave him. 'You were off delivering a baby, and from the description I received on the phone it sounded as though it needed suturing.'

He stopped and pointed to the lounge. 'Wouldn't you like to sit down? This is quite a story.'

'You're telling me,' Sarah muttered, standing exactly

where she was. Ren simply smiled, placed his hands on her shoulders and forced her rigid frame to sit.

'When they arrived, and I'd managed to get little Jimmy to stop wailing at the top of his lungs, I took a closer look at his eye. The horn had hit him just above the eyebrow and the skin was intact. He'd also been fortunate enough to have screwed his eyes tightly shut before the blood covered his face.

'All I was doing when you walked in was cleaning him up. Then I sent him and his relieved parents on their way. That's it. End of story. If it had been Edith in there cleaning him up, I bet you wouldn't be this mad at her,' he pointed out logically, sitting down next to her.

'Now, why don't I take you over to the pub for a drink so you can relax from your tiring day.' He reached out a hand and began massaging her neck.

Sarah's body convulsed into life as though it had been lying dormant, just waiting for his touch. Springing to her feet to break the contact, she glared down at him.

'No, thank you,' she forced out politely. 'I have paperwork to catch up on but, before I go, I have one more question for you. If your hire car doesn't arrive until tomorrow where are you going to sleep tonight?'

'What's wrong with the spare bed?' he asked innocently.

'Dammit, Ren. You know what I mean. Have you given any consideration to what the townspeople will say when they find out you're staying here? Last night would probably have been acceptable, considering the emergency, but to remain here will start the rumours flying thick and fast. Think of my reputation. Not only as a doctor but as a single woman.'

'Does this mean you're asking me to stay on longer?' Ren gave her an ironic smile.

'Aagh,' she seethed and strode out of the room. He caught up with her in the doorway to her consulting room.

'To be completely honest, I really like this town. I had a good look around it today and consider it the perfect place for me to rest, recuperate and relax. To really unwind. You know how stressful life in a hospital can be.'

'Yes, I do,' she said and turned to face him. 'And it can be just as stressful as a country practice with an annoying orthopaedic surgeon hanging around.'

He grinned at her, his thumbs stuck in the pockets of his jeans as he relaxed against the doorframe. He exuded sexual charm and its full potency seemed to be aimed at Sarah. . .and it was working.

'Oh, all right,' she gave in. Anything to get him to move away from her. She felt her body tingle as she saw that slow smile, which was becoming familiar to her, spread across his handsome face.

'All right. . .what?'

'You can stay. But just for tonight, then I would like you to leave and never come back. Do you understand?'

'You're the boss.' He pushed himself away from the doorframe and walked off toward the kitchen.

Frustrated at his nonchalance, Sarah resisted the impulse to slam the door and, instead, directed her energies to her work.

It was over an hour later that she finally began to relax, absorbed in her work. She whistled tunelessly as she updated her supply lists and faxed off orders to the appropriate companies. She was just tidying her desk when there was a knock at the door. Edith poked her head round and smiled.

'Is it dinnertime already?' Sarah quickly glanced at

the clock. 'Time flies when you're having fun,' she said with a smile and walked over to the door. 'What delights are you going to spoil me with tonight?'

'I've made a fresh lasagne and tossed a salad. You need to keep your cholesterol down and your nutrients up,' Edith lectured, not for the first time.

'With you looking after me, how can I not eat anything but balanced meals?' Sarah laughed and rounded the corner into the kitchen. The table was set, complete with tablecloth, side plates, linen serviettes, wine glasses and candles.

Sarah turned an accusing look on Edith. 'What's all this for?'

'Well, you are entertaining a man, aren't you?' Edith at least had the grace to look a little contrite.

'No, I am not,' Sarah stated emphatically, and Ren chose that moment to join them.

'I'll leave you to it. The salad's in the fridge, along with the wine. The lasagne and bread are in the oven, keeping warm. See you both tomorrow.' Edith quickly scurried out of the room.

'That woman,' Sarah muttered and turned to the fridge. She took out the salad and wine, then looked over at Ren. 'Well, don't just stand there. Get the things out of the oven.'

'Right.' He jumped to it.

Sarah obstinately removed the candles from the table, deciding that they had made the atmosphere more intimate. Edith had obviously gone to a lot of trouble because the bread was freshly baked and the wine a nice Australian claret.

They ate in a relatively comfortable silence for a while before Ren remarked, 'I love Italian food.' He ate another bite, before raising his fingers to his lips and kissing the air the way Italians did. 'Edith is a brilliant cook but I never expected her to make a fresh lasagne just for me.'

'What do you mean?' Sarah asked cautiously.

'She came over earlier this morning while you were out delivering babies. We had a pleasant chat and the topic of food came up. She asked me what I liked best and I told her. Then, faster than you can say "*Eccola*!", fresh Italian food appears on the table.'

'How did she know you were going to be here? You were supposed to leave,' Sarah said pointedly.

'No. The car was supposed to be delivered and she made me promise this morning that I would stay until after dinner. When she brought the food across just now I informed her of the further change in my plans.'

Sarah couldn't talk because of the rage that was seething inside her. Instead she nodded her head, acknowledging his comments. How could Edith betray her like this? OK, so she'd told Sarah that she liked Ren but that didn't mean that she had to get all chummy-chummy with him. Then, on the other hand, the table had been set as though for a romantic meal.

She promised herself to have a stern talk with her surrogate mother at the first available opportunity. Trying to match her up with a man she didn't like was meddling in her private affairs. It wasn't the first time Edith had tried and it certainly wouldn't be the last but, damn the woman, she had to learn to let Sarah pick her own Mr Right.

'Does Edith usually cook for you?' Ren asked, interrupting Sarah's thoughts.

'Yes.'

'Is that because you *can't* cook?'

'No. It's just her way of showing that she loves me,'

Sarah said softly. The annoyance she'd felt toward Edith only moments ago vanished.

Ren stopped eating and looked at her. She could feel his gaze and slowly she raised her eyes to meet his. 'What is it now?'

'I was just thinking how nice it would be to have someone like Edith caring for me.' He spoke so quietly that Sarah barely heard him. Frowning, she wondered if this was another attempt at his weird sarcasm, but his expression held a hint of vulnerability.

'Sorry,' he said, lightening the mood. 'I didn't mean to wax rhapsodic. I'll do the dishes, if you like.'

'OK.' Sarah's voice cracked and she quickly cleared her throat. She pressed her fingers to her temple, trying to ease the beginning of a headache brought on by her emotions being on a roller-coaster ride.

Ren removed their plates and carried them over to the bench.

'Don't sprain a finger loading the dishwasher and turning it on,' she said wearily, managing a grin, and for the first time she was rewarded with a genuine smile.

Their gaze held across the kitchen, the dirty dishes between them. The electricity that was sparking around the room would have been enough to light the whole town. Thank heaven she'd removed those candles and the potential atmosphere they had created.

Wetting her suddenly dry lips, Sarah stood. 'I think I'll have an early night. It's been an. . .unusual day.'

'Sure. I'll lock the house up. Goodnight, Sarah.'

Walking into her room, she shut the door and leant against it. What on earth was happening between them? He wasn't her type. And, apart from that, she didn't even *like* him!

*   *   *

Sarah always woke early on Monday mornings and this Monday was no exception. When she entered the kitchen after a quick shower she found Ren, standing by the stove and cooking bacon and eggs.

'You're practically right where I left you last night,' Sarah attempted to joke. She still didn't like the idea of him staying in her home and here he was, helping himself to her food. But, she reasoned with herself, he would be gone by this afternoon and she wouldn't have to worry any more. In the meantime, she could at least be civil to him.

'Let me assure you that I have slept and that I'm raring to go. How do you like your eggs?' He turned to face her, giving her that aggravating grin of his.

She had a sudden insight. He was *expecting* her to flare up at his question. Well, she wouldn't give him the satisfaction.

'I don't usually have a cooked breakfast but, considering all the trouble you've gone to, I like them sunny side up.' Sarah busied herself with setting the table while Ren finished cooking.

As they ate he quizzed her about the town. Sarah lovingly spouted its history and in the process revealed some of her own.

'So you worked at the Royal Hobart Hospital as well?' He seemed genuinely surprised.

'Yes. I did my internship rotation there.'

'Why didn't you go into practice in the city? You could make a lot more money.'

Sarah visibly bristled at his suggestion but held herself in check. 'True, but money isn't everything. Besides, this town and surrounding district needed a doctor. Country folk can get just as sick as city folk.'

'Oh, I don't dispute that fact at all.' Ren stood and

cleared the table and Sarah felt as though she'd just been put through some kind of test. 'So, boss. What's on the agenda for today?' He came to stand beside her.

'I don't know what you're doing but I've got house calls this morning and clinic this afternoon.' She stood, turned her back on him and went to her consulting room. Checking her list of files and packing the necessary medication into her black doctor's bag, Sarah whistled while she worked.

She could hear the shower running and instantly her imagination began to run wild. Ren. Naked. Across the hallway! Sarah sat down in her chair and closed her eyes. She had no trouble at all in picturing his torso as she'd seen it before. She imagined his tanned muscles being lathered with soap, his black hair plastered to his head as he let the water spray over him.

She could visualise all too clearly droplets of water forming on those firm masculine shoulders, settling there for an instant before making their way through the smattering of dark hair that covered his chest— down over his washboard stomach before cascading toward his thighs. Then the sound of the water stopped.

Sarah sighed and ran trembling fingers through her hair. Her pulse was pounding rapidly and she concentrated on her breathing, forcing it to a steadier pace.

Her breathing was almost back to normal when the fax machine which was located directly behind her desk squealed its high-pitched tone, almost sending her through the roof with fright. When had she become so jumpy? Ren was really beginning to get to her—in more ways than one—and the sooner he left the better.

The fax machine ended its transmission and Sarah snatched the paper off the tray to read it. She scanned

it twice, before scrunching it into a tightly wadded ball
and throwing it at her wall.

'Damn him!' she said vehemently.

'Damn who?' Ren's voice came from her open doorway and she looked up in surprise. He was wearing a
royal blue polo shirt with a pair of old blue jeans which
had long since forgotten any shape but his. Sarah
quickly scanned his body again, before meeting
his gaze.

The blueness of his shirt made his eyes more vibrant,
hypnotising her back into fantasy land. His dark hair
was combed neatly into place and Sarah could smell
the freshness of his scent as he walked toward her.

'You like?' He raised an eyebrow at her and grinned
wolfishly. Sarah broke eye contact and cleared her
throat.

'Sorry, what did you say?' She frowned at him as
though purposely misunderstanding him.

'I asked who you were damning now.' He bent and
retrieved the crumbled fax, before lobbing it into
the bin.

Sarah slumped into her chair. 'Just some creep of a
professor in Hobart.' Her head shot up and she looked at
him. 'You'd know him. The professor of Orthopaedics.'

Ren simply nodded. 'What's the problem?'

'Now he's away for the next two weeks. Before that
he was overseas and before that at a meeting or in
surgery or consulting or probably playing two hundred
holes of golf. I've been trying to track him down for
the past two months but his Trojan of a secretary always
gives me some kind of excuse.'

'Maybe he's genuinely busy,' Ren pointed out.

'As doctors, we're all busy,' Sarah countered. 'That
doesn't mean he can't give me ten minutes of his time

to hear what I have to say. All I want is a chance to speak to him face to face.' She thumped her fist on the desk. 'I'd have more luck raising money so I could walk to the moon than of seeing him. Crotchety "old Hound".' Sarah scrunched up her nose in disgust as she used the Professor's nickname.

Ren eyed her quizzically. 'What did you call him?'

'The "old Hound". You know, Professor Fox-Taylor. Fox and Hound. As one of his staff, I thought you would know it.'

'Must have escaped my ears. How do you know about it?' Ren's voice remained calm but a smile tugged at his lips.

'A friend of mine works in the reconstructive surgery department and he told me. I've never met the man but apparently he insists on being called by his full title by everyone. Professor Fox-Taylor. He must still be in the Dark Ages, not letting people call him Prof or even by his first name. I'm so glad I didn't do my orthopaedic rotation under *his* guidance.'

'Why?'

'Because I just know we would have clashed on every single point brought up for discussion. Arguing your way through a rotation is not the best way to pass it, believe me.'

Ren chuckled. 'You sound as though you're talking from experience.'

'I am.' She nodded miserably.

'So, what is it you so desperately want to see the "old Hound" about?'

Sarah eyed Ren suspiciously, but he waved away her scepticism by saying, 'I don't mean to pry but, as an orthopaedic colleague, maybe I can put in a good word for you.'

She sighed. 'It's just an idea I've had.'

'Well, tell me what it is.' Ren waited patiently while Sarah weighed up the pros and cons of revealing her secret to him.

'OK. While I was working in Africa. . .'

'Really? When?' He seemed genuinely interested.

'Just before I came back to Australia. I was in Europe for three years, working in various countries—picking up a bit of locum work here and there. Then two years doing volunteer work in Africa. Anyway, I had to do a bit of orthopaedics, among other things, as I was the only doctor for five different villages. The nearest hospital was at least a two-day walk.

'I needed to perform an emergency hip operation, and with the crude second-hand tools that I had I rigged up a special jig to help me stabilise an area once I'd worked on it. Since I've been back I've had a prototype made and want the old Hound's opinion on whether it's marketable or not.'

'May I see it?' Ren had sat quietly through her speech, only nodding every now and then.

'It's not here. I'm expecting it in some time later this week, along with my next delivery of medical supplies from Hobart.' The phone on her desk shrilled to life and Sarah quickly answered it, severing any further conversation regarding her jig. She noticed that Ren didn't bother to hide his interest as he sat there and listened to her conversation.

'Fine, Mrs Birch. I'll drop in and see you at ten o'clock. Bye for now.' Sarah replaced the receiver and immediately hunted out some nitroglycerin tablets and put them in her bag.

'I'd better go or I'll end up running late all day. Edith brings lunch over around one, and I'm sure there'll be plenty for you as well,' Sarah said as she clipped her mobile phone onto her jeans.

Ren stood and picked up her bag.

'It's OK. I can manage.' Sarah held out her hand for the bag.

'It's no trouble, considering I'm going with you on your rounds.'

'Oh, no, you're not. You've already invaded my house as well as my personal privacy. I will *not* allow you to interfere with my patients.'

'Want to arm-wrestle for it?' Ren grinned at her and Sarah threw her arms up in disgust and walked out of the door.

'Why do you have to argue about everything?' Ren asked good-naturedly as he followed her out to the car.

Sarah rounded on him and stood with her hands planted firmly on her hips. 'Why do *you* have to keep intruding into my life?' She turned and wrenched open the door. 'I don't want you to come,' she said firmly when he was seated beside her, 'but what I want or don't want doesn't seem to make any difference as far as you're concerned. You are the most arrogant, imposing, demanding and infuriating man I have ever had the misfortune to meet.'

She clipped her seat belt and turned the ignition key. The engine sprang to life and, dropping the clutch, she took off, out onto the dusty road.

'You know,' he remarked casually as he buckled his belt, 'you should be a red head.'

'That's just the kind of stereotypical comment I'd expect from you,' Sarah snapped. She resumed the pose of ignoring him but she was sure that he didn't realise it, and that infuriated her even more.

'Where's your first stop?'

'The baby I delivered yesterday.' She would treat him as she would any other doctor who had come into town for a visit. With polite indifference.

Fifteen minutes later, she pulled off the road into a dirt drive that wound its way to the Dumar homestead. Sarah brought the vehicle to a stop and jumped to the ground, leaving Ren to follow and to carry her bag.

Knocking on the hard, wooden door, she waited for Lizzie to answer. No reply. Sarah knocked again and tried the handle. It was unlocked and she ventured inside.

'Hello?' Sarah called and followed the sounds of a crying baby, which were coming from the rear of the house. 'Lizzie? It's Sarah,' she called. She found Lizzie sitting on the edge of the unmade bed, her face buried in her hands and little Reuben lying on the bed beside her, screaming his head off.

Sarah picked the infant up and cuddled him. Slowly his sobs subsided. While he was temporarily quiet, and to give Lizzie some time to get herself together, Sarah read the notes Kate had left for her and examined the baby. His eyes, ears and nose seemed fine. She checked his organs, rotation, reflexes and his umbilical cord. She noted all her findings in his notes for Kate, who should return within the hour.

Naturally Reuben started roaring his head off when Sarah began to poke and prod him and when she was finished she noticed Ren lounging in the doorway. She carried the babe over to him.

'Hold him, please,' she asked softly. For an instant, Sarah watched as the little chap snuggled contentedly into Ren's chest and closed his eyes. Amazed, she looked at him and smiled. He winked at her before he carried Reuben off, talking to him quietly.

'Having a rotten time?' Sarah asked sympathetically, and sat down beside the woman who was only a few years younger than herself.

'He hasn't stopped crying since Kate left last night and I'm so very tired. I've fed him, bathed him, changed him, cuddled him and he still keeps on crying.' Fresh tears sprang into her eyes. 'I never thought it would be this bad. John got no sleep last night and left earlier than usual to tend to the animals. I didn't even have time to prepare his breakfast,' Lizzie sniffled.

Sarah reached for the box of tissues on the dresser and held one out to Lizzie. 'Why didn't you call me? Or Kate?'

'I don't know. Just look at me,' she said, and held her arms out wide for Sarah to see. 'I can't even find the time to have a shower and get dressed because he keeps crying.'

Sarah put an arm around the other woman's shoulders. 'Tell you what. Dr Taylor and I will look after Reuben while you have a shower and breakfast. How does that sound?'

Lizzie gave Sarah a watery smile. 'Do you have the time?'

'Of course.' Sarah smiled. 'Now go and get in that shower and I'll put the kettle on.'

Lizzie gratefully did as she was told and Sarah went to find Ren. He was standing, looking at some pictures on the mantel, little Reuben settled and asleep in his arms. He turned when he heard her.

'I've sent her off for a shower. It's such a change from her normal daily routine that naturally it will take her a while to adjust. Her mother is due to fly in from Canada next week so I'll arrange more support for her until then.'

'Where's her husband?'

'Out working. The farm is their living and he can't stop his work to stay here and help, even if he wanted to.'

'But surely he could have waited long enough for Lizzie to have a shower?'

'Apparently not,' Sarah said sadly.

'What happened to the sensitive new-age guy?' Ren asked as he continued to gently rock Reuben in his arms.

'You're the male. You tell me.' Sarah smiled. Ren followed her into the kitchen and sat down. His legs were long enough, and Reuben small enough, to lie the baby on his knees.

'How's Lizzie feeling, otherwise?' he enquired as he watched Sarah move around the kitchen.

'I haven't had a chance to examine her but I imagine she's not feeling too good.'

Ren glanced down briefly at his watch. 'Where's your next stop?'

'Mrs Birch at ten. You'll like her.' Sarah grinned wickedly and Ren raised an eyebrow.

'Why is that?'

'She just *loves* bachelors. Lucky for you she's just married off the last of her five daughters.' Sarah placed a cup of coffee in front of him and sat down opposite. 'Are you comfortable with Reuben on your knee or would you like me to put him down?'

'He's fine. Let the little chap rest.'

Lizzie came into the kitchen, looking much better, and Sarah quickly introduced her to Ren.

'Oh, yes. I vaguely remember hearing about that emergency the other night and how you were staying at Sarah's,' Lizzie remarked matter-of-factly, and Sarah sent Ren a pointed look as if to say, I told you people would gossip.

'What would you like for breakfast?' Sarah said, rising to her feet and forcing Lizzie down into a chair.

'Just coffee and toast are about all I could face.' She glanced across at Ren, then looked down at her sleeping son. 'He really is such a beautiful baby but I'm so at a loss. . .' She let her words trail off.

'That's natural,' Ren said, his voice soft and radiating sincerity. 'You've gone from being a wife to being a wife *and* a mother within a few short hours. Not only do you have a husband who depends heavily upon you, but you now also have a helpless infant who will rely on you for absolutely every little thing for at least the next twenty years or so.'

Sarah placed the toast and coffee in front of Lizzie who seemed to be listening intently to Ren. He seemed to have a hypnotising effect on everyone he met. . .except her.

He'd been here less than forty-eight hours and yet Trevor and Edith, two people whose opinion she valued most, thought he was wonderful. Now he could add Lizzie and little Reuben to his fan club. She was also sure that Mrs Birch would be willing to walk over hot coals for him by the time they left her.

'It feels as though your son needs changing, so, while Sarah examines you, I'll change the little chap's nappy.' The women watched as he expertly gathered the small bundle into his arms and walked out of the room.

'Oh, Sarah,' Lizzie gushed. 'He's just wonderful. And that gorgeous English accent would make any woman's bones turn to jelly. Why, if I wasn't a happily married woman, I'd steal him away from you.'

Well, Sarah thought. He's certainly brightened up

Lizzie's day. 'I hate to disappoint you but there is nothing, absolutely nothing, between us. Besides, he's leaving today and going back to Hobart.'

'Sure,' Lizzie said, her voice radiating disbelief. 'Anyone seeing the two of you together can see the electricity crackle between you.' She giggled girlishly and began eating her toast.

Really? Could people *really* see the chemistry between them? Sarah had felt it and didn't deny it, but Ren just wasn't her type. Was he?

CHAPTER THREE

SARAH pushed Lizzie's insinuations out of her mind and concentrated on the examination. Lizzie was exhibiting all the healthy signs and symptoms that a new mother should.

'Try to lie down yourself when he goes to sleep. If you don't keep your strength up then neither will he,' Sarah said as they walked down the front steps. 'Did Kate say what time she would be back?'

'She said she would be back by ten.'

'Good.' Sarah glanced at her watch. 'It's almost that now. I'll be around same time tomorrow morning to check on you.' She and Ren climbed into the car and waved as they took off down the driveway. They were both silent as Sarah pulled onto the main road and headed toward Mrs Birch's house.

'Isn't there a district nurse to serve this community?' Ren asked quietly, and Sarah shook her head.

'There's Kate and myself and, as far as the government's concerned, that's enough. Some of the neighbouring communities only have a district nurse. Sometimes I'll see patients, if they want to travel this far, but most of the time it's easier for them to go to up to Launceston or down to Hobart. In dire emergencies, and if I'm the closest doctor, Trevor flies me where I need to go.'

'You need more help, Sarah. You're doing all the little fiddly things like postnatal check-ups, and not leaving yourself enough time for general practitioner work.'

'I don't mind doing all the fiddly things,' she said starchily, and she heard him sigh in exasperation.

'I wasn't criticising you, I was commending you. You seem to love your job. . .'

'I do.'

'But a district nurse and possibly another doctor would make all the difference to this ever-growing community. Kate seems so reluctant to do anything that it's a wonder you cope at all. Which is why I've decided to stay.'

'What!'

'At least for the next few weeks. I have plenty of vacation time and I couldn't think of a better way of spending it.'

'No way,' Sarah argued desperately as she turned into Mrs Birch's drive, which was lined with masses of beautiful flowers. 'You said you were going this afternoon and I want you gone.' She pulled to a stop and, taking a deep breath, turned in her seat to look at him.

'I admit that you were a great help with Lizzie and I want to thank you. I've let you tag along this morning. . .'

'For which I humbly thank you,' he interjected sardonically, both of them knowing full well that her words were a lie.

'But dammit, Ren. This is my life and I don't want you in it. Go back to Hobart, *please*, and do whatever it is that you do. Now come on before Mrs Birch gets in a tizz about her morning tea being ruined.'

'Morning tea?' she heard him mumble as they walked to the door. Mrs Birch opened it before they could

knock and seemed delighted at having male company
as well.

'What a handsome young man you are, Dr Taylor,'
she giggled after Sarah had introduced them. 'Please
sit down while I fetch another cup and saucer.' She
quickly hurried from the room and Ren turned to glare
at Sarah.

'I thought she was a patient?' he said in a harsh
whisper.

'She is,' Sarah replied, seating herself in a delicate
Regency chair. 'Angina pectoris, but she loves to enter-
tain so when I call we always have morning or afternoon
tea.' Sarah motioned for Ren to sit and grinned at him
sweetly. 'You see, although I may be very busy, the
people appreciate me and definitely look after me.'

'Here we are.' Mrs Birch returned and placed a dainty
cup, saucer and plate in front of Ren. The table held a
lavish spread of freshly baked scones, with jam and
cream beside them, home-made cakes and biscuits—as
well as milk, sugar and tea, which was brewing in Mrs
Birch's best teapot.

'You should have told me, Sarah, dear, that you were
bringing a friend,' Mrs Birch scolded and Sarah
shrugged as she helped herself to a scone.

'I'm sorry, but it was a last-minute decision for Dr
Taylor to accompany me on my visiting rounds.'

'And did you see young Lizzie Dumar?'

'Yes. She was our first call. Little Reuben is a delight-
fully healthy baby and I'm sure Lizzie would appreciate
any support the townsfolk can give her,' Sarah replied
as she sipped her tea. She couldn't resist a glance at
Ren but amazingly enough his large hands didn't look
clumsy around the small handle of the cup.

'Certainly,' Mrs Birch replied, before turning her

attention to Ren. 'I have nine grandchildren . . .' she reached out and touched Ren's hand '. . .and my youngest daughter has, finally, just got married. It was such a lovely wedding and all of my grandchildren were involved. Would you like to see the photographs, Dr Taylor?' Mrs Birch rose from the table before Ren could answer and quickly fetched a large album.

He gave Sarah a pained looked but she just grinned and helped herself to another scone. It was almost fifteen minutes later that Sarah decided to take pity on him, after watching him show a polite interest in Mrs Birch's family.

'I think that's enough excitement for the morning,' Sarah scolded gently and reached for the photo album. 'I brought you some more nitroglycerin tablets so—if you would like to go to your bedroom—we'll proceed with the examination.'

'Sarah Rutherford. . .' Mrs Birch shook a finger at her but nevertheless did as she was told '. . .you always were a bossy child.' She looked at Ren and said conspiratorially, 'She may look just like her mother but she's definitely got her father's temperament.'

Sarah examined Mrs Birch thoroughly, taking blood samples to test her cholesterol, platelet and glucose levels. 'Everything else seems fine and I'll let you know the results of these tests next week.'

Ren was patiently waiting in the front room when Sarah returned. Mrs Birch tried to offer them another cup of tea and Ren quickly declined. Sarah was amused at his attitude but reiterated his stand.

'We must get to our next appointment, Mrs Birch, but you come and see me in the clinic if you have any problems.'

'I will, dear. Did you know, Dr Taylor, that our Sarah

is a brilliant doctor?' Mrs Birch continued to chatter as Sarah led the way out of the house.

'So I've seen,' Ren answered noncommitally.

'Her father was as proud as punch the day she graduated and although he couldn't fly to Melbourne to be with her we had a slap-up party at his house to celebrate.'

'I'm sure it was delightful.' Ren opened the passenger door and climbed in.

'I bet poor Joe would have loved to see his little Sarah get married.' She gave Sarah a hopeful look, before gesturing to Ren. 'Any chance it will be soon, dear?'

'Not yet, Mrs Birch.' Sarah smiled and waved, before reversing and turning onto the road. She glanced at Ren and chuckled. 'I told you Mrs Birch would take a shine to you.'

'Whew! I didn't think I was going to get out of there alive. Right, boss. Where's the next stop?'

'Old Mrs Mac's dump yard. If you thought you had it easy with Mrs Birch, wait until you meet Bertie MacPhail. She'll eat you alive.'

'Maybe you should just drop me at your place,' he said, feigning panic.

'No way, Ren Taylor. You insisted on coming with me so there's no backing out now.'

Ren took in his surroundings. 'Aren't we headed back toward the Dumar farm?'

'Yes. Mrs MacPhail lives beyond Lizzie and John.'

'Well, why didn't you go there earlier?'

'I thought the answer to that would be obvious.' She waited for Ren to shrug, before patiently explaining. 'Morning tea just isn't morning tea if it isn't served by ten. If I'd gone to Bertie's after Lizzie's we'd have had to eat lunch with Mrs Birch.'

'Good heavens, no!'

'And lunch takes twice as long as morning tea.' Sarah chuckled and this time Ren joined in.

'You're a wise woman, Sarah.'

'Then you'll listen to me when I ask you not to stay?'

He sighed at her words and frowned. 'Don't flog a dead horse. We'll discuss it after your clinic this afternoon. So, tell me more about Mrs MacPhail and why you call her home the dump yard?' he asked in an attempt to resurrect the friendly rapport they'd had since leaving Mrs Birch.

'As a child, I was always petrified of her. Probably because she's always been old and wrinkly and grumpy since the first time I saw her. Her husband was involved in a gruesome tractor accident over forty years ago. Bertie was the one who found him, hauled his body back near the house, dug his grave and buried him.

'The whole town was abuzz with rumours that are still repeated over how she killed him, which made us kids even more scared of her.'

'And did she?' Ren seemed riveted at her story.

'No one ever knew for sure but since I've come to know her I've realised that there is no way in the world that that lady would harm anyone, although she'd certainly give you cause to suspect.' Sarah grinned at him but continued with her story.

'She's eighty-six years old and as tough as nails. And don't you go telling anyone her age as she swore me to secrecy when I told her I needed it for medical purposes. Don't forget, you're bound by the same confidentiality clauses as I am.'

'You have my word. In fact, I've already forgotten
how old she is.'

'Good.' Sarah nodded with satisfaction. 'The reason
we call her place the dump yard is because that's exactly
what it looks like. I remember when my father brought
me out here when I was about seven. I honestly thought
the MacPhail farm was where old machinery went
to die.

'To a seven-year-old the place looked so scary, with
old tractors and cars lying everywhere. Tyres, bicycles
and bits of debris littered the yard. My father and Bertie
had been friends for as long as anyone could remember.
No romance between them at all—just friends. Dad
persuaded Bertie to get rid of some of the junk from
her yard, and when she finally agreed he arranged for
the machinery to be sold to a motor museum and for
the townfolk to lend a hand in helping to clean the
yard up.

'It doesn't look nearly as bad as it did all those years
ago, and the money raised cleared the debt on the farm
so that Bertie could live there without any worries.'
Sarah turned off and headed up the drive. 'Mike Jayton,
whom you met the other night, comes out here weekly
to tend to Bertie's front and back lawns. Edith organised
a roster of women to come once a day to bring Bertie
a meal and help clean the place up.'

'So, apart from being overly frightening, what's
wrong with her?'

'She has glaucoma. I've been trying to persuade her
to go to Hobart for day surgery and have laser treatment
to reduce the pressure, but she's as stubborn as a mule.'
Sarah came to a stop and reached over into the back
seat for a wicker basket.

'Where did that come from?' Ren asked as he

took a peek inside. 'Is that pumpkin pie?'

'Yes. Edith would have baked this last night and Trevor would have put it in the car early this morning. I always come out on Mondays. It's my rostered day.'

'And what if you can't make it? What if you're too busy playing doctor to adhere to the roster?'

Sarah shrugged nonchalantly. 'Then Edith comes instead. Look over there.' She pointed to an enormous gum tree. 'That's where she buried her husband, and every day she goes over and has a rest against the trunk.'

Ren shook his head in amazement. 'You're certainly a weird bunch out here.'

'Come on, or would you rather stay put?' she challenged as she walked up the front steps.

Sarah knocked once, before opening the door and walking in. 'Bertie, it's Sarah,' she called, and continued on her way into the kitchen.

A short, plump, grey-haired woman, with extremely thick glasses, appeared from a side door. 'What'd ya want?' she growled but let Sarah give her withered cheek a kiss.

'It's Monday and that's doctor day, so here I am.' Sarah unloaded the pie from the basket and switched the oven on to reheat it.

'Who's he?' Bertie stabbed an arthritic finger in Ren's direction.

'This is Dr Taylor. He's visiting from Hobart. Now behave yourself and go and get your eye drops.'

'Bossy little runt,' Bertie mumbled as she turned her back on them and shuffled up the hallway. 'If it weren't for ya father. . .' she called clearly over her shoulder, and Sarah mimicked the words as though she'd heard them a hundred times before. Ren could hardly keep from laughing out loud. '. . .I wouldn't let ya behave

in such a way in me own home. Always meddlin', ya
do-gooder.'

Sarah grinned and raised her eyebrows in an I-told-
you-so gesture at Ren, before turning her attention to
the dishes in the sink. Running the water, she usually
left them to soak until Bertie had finished eating
her lunch.

The old woman returned and Sarah sat her down at
the table. 'Have you put all your drops in?' Sarah
removed Bertie's glasses and set them on the table.

'Ya ask me the same question every time. Of course I
have, pesky things that they are. I don't have a second's
peace, without havin' ta put in a drop of somethin'
or other.'

Sarah put a few drops of anaesthetic into each eye
and withdrew her ophthalmoscope from her bag. She
needed to wait for the anaesthetic to take effect before
she checked the pressure. 'Well, if you'd have that
painless, very minor operation I keep nagging you about
then you wouldn't have to put as many drops in,' Sarah
couldn't resist teasing.

'Fair dinkum, Sarah. Ya do go on. Ya've got the
whole townsfolk babbling on about this operation. I
can't turn a corner or have a visitor come round without
it bein' mentioned.'

'It's for your own good,' Sarah reiterated. Edith was
right. Peer pressure was the only way to get to Bertie
MacPhail. 'If my father were here he'd be nagging you
just the same as I do.'

'Sarah's right,' Ren chimed in. 'I work at the Royal
Hobart Hospital and can assure you that the operation
only takes a few hours, and then you can be on your
way home again.'

'Oh, for heaven's sake,' Bertie snarled and pulled

away from Sarah's touch to glare, as best she could, at Ren. 'If we'd wanted the pig we'd have rattled the bucket!'

Sarah turned the old woman's chin back to face her and continued with her examination.

'Blasted outsiders. Think they know everthin',' Bertie mumbled. Sarah glanced over at Ren, whose face had a white pallor, and winked at him.

'Don't you go picking on Ren,' Sarah scolded. 'He's a highly respectable surgeon, who could probably make your trip to Hobart a lot easier by pulling a few strings.' She reached for her Perkins tonometer to measure the pressure of the aqueous humour in each eye. 'Now hold still, Bertie.'

'I can't do anythin' with him watchin'.'

'Oh, be quiet. He's a doctor as well and, besides, you can't even see him. He's come to help me and you should be grateful. Now be a good girl and hold still,' Sarah placated her firmly.

'If it weren't for ya father. . .' Bertie mumbled but, nevertheless, sat still.

'Any problems with further loss of focusing power?'

'A bit.'

'How about at night? Any changes?'

'Maybe.'

'Any pain?'

'Some.'

'Right, then,' Sarah put her instruments away. She knew that Bertie never told her the truth regarding the amount of pain she might be in, and the fact that Bertie had confessed to actually feeling *some* was an indication that this operation was definitely needed. 'Off to your bedroom so I can check the rest of you.'

'There's nothin' wrong with me, I tell ya.'

'Stop making excuses and go.' Sarah met Ren's eyes and rolled her own heavenwards. 'We go through this routine every single time, and every single time she complains and whinges.'

'Watch ya mouth, girlie. Ya ain't too old for me ta put ya over my knee.'

Sarah laughed. 'I may not be too old but I'd certainly be too heavy. Come on.' She helped the old lady out of the chair, then smiled wickedly at Ren and winked. 'Maybe, when I've finished, Dr Taylor can have a look at your arthritic fingers.'

'Certainly,' Ren said.

'Thank you. It would be good to get an expert's opinion on them. In the meantime, you can start on the dishes.'

'Right you are.'

And, to Sarah's surprise, he did just that—but not before he'd poked his tongue out at her.

They were back in ten minutes, and Bertie behaved herself while Ren examined her hands and checked her range of motion.

'They look fine to me, although I think we may need to amputate in the not too distant future.' He made sure that his voice radiated with humour, and Bertie playfully slapped his hand away.

'Get away with ya, ya pesky outsider.' But her voice held none of the malice it had earlier and a grin split her face.

After they'd fed Bertie and cleaned the house Sarah and Ren said their goodbyes.

'I wouldn't bother with the likes of 'im, if I were you, Sarah. Not good enough for ya.'

'Thanks for the advice, Bertie,' Sarah said, revving the engine to life. 'See you later.'

Sarah wound down the window once they were onto the sealed road and let the breeze blow about the car, thankful that her hair was short enough not to flick back into her face.

'I'm curious, Sarah,' Ren said, and seemed to be choosing his words carefully. 'Why didn't you set Bertie or Mrs Birch straight regarding our relationship?'

'What's the point?' She shrugged. She couldn't in any way, shape or form let him know that those comments had aggravated her. If he hadn't insisted on staying in her home the insinuations might never have been voiced.

'To defend your honour?'

'In a small country town? Get real, Ren. People will gossip, regardless of the circumstances, and anything that I say to the contrary will add fuel to the fire. I've found that if you ignore the gossip it eventually stops.'

He nodded his head in thoughtful agreement. 'Where's the next stop?'

'Home. It's lunchtime and I'm ravenous.'

As Sarah had predicted, Edith had sent over enough food to feed them both—and then some. Patients for her afternoon clinic were already arriving as Sarah quickly ate the last few mouthfuls of her salad.

'I'm surprised that you don't put on any weight with the amount of food you eat,' Ren commented as she drained the dregs of her drink. 'Then again, with the amount of running around you seem to do, I can understand why the calories don't have enough time to settle in.' He gave her body a leisurely appraisal as he spoke and Sarah felt as though it were his fingers, not just his eyes, that had touched her deep within and left her smouldering with desire.

She tried to speak but found her vocal cords were

not being co-operative. Clearing her throat, she tried again. 'I'd better start the clinic or I'll be working until midnight.' Without waiting for an answer, she quickly turned and left him sitting at the kitchen table.

Entering the bathroom, she splashed cold water on her face before she gave her reflection a stern lecture regarding the man who had casually intruded into her life.

The clinic ran smoothly, with only minor complaints and check-ups. She hardly had time to wonder what Ren was up to while she was busy with her patients.

'Margaret, please sit down,' Sarah said, closing the door behind her last patient. 'How's everything at home?'

'Fine, Sarah.'

'How are Paul and the children?'

'They're all fine.' Margaret nervously clutched her handbag and glanced, wide-eyed, across the desk at Sarah.

Sarah found it hard to believe that Margaret was the same age as herself. She looked at least ten years older, but with six children under the age of twelve she really had her hands full.

'I've received the results of your tests, and your hae-moglobin is low. It's not low enough for a transfusion, thank goodness, but I'll put you on iron tablets and see how they go.' Sarah watched the panic cross over Margaret's face.

'We need to try conservative treatment for your fibroids, before even contemplating whether surgery is necessary. If it is, you may even need to have a hysterec-tomy. I don't want to alarm you unnecessarily but you need to know all the facts. As I've explained to you before fibroids are benign tumours, consisting of fibrous and muscle tissue, that grow in the wall of the womb. Your symptoms of pain and clotting while menstruating, as well as pressure on the bladder, are all consistent with this diagnosis.' Sarah made sure that her voice was calm and matter-of-fact. 'You can elect to have them removed, but the decision is yours. I can only advise you.'

When Margaret's chin began to wobble and tears to flood her eyes Sarah came around from behind her desk to sit next to her. Cradling an arm across her shoulders, Sarah soothed and reassured while the other woman softly cried.

Blowing her nose, Margaret looked up at Sarah. 'I haven't been having as many cramps as before and the other pains seemed to have settled down.'

'In view of what I've told you today, why don't you go home and discuss the situation with Paul? He's coped marvellously in the past when you've had to go to Hobart, and the three older children are very responsible.'

Again Margaret's lip began to quiver but she bravely held herself together.

'If you decided to have surgery you'll be able to have a relaxing holiday, with your mum and aunty fussy over you and paying you lots of attention.'

Margaret managed a watery smile and nodded. 'I'll discuss it with Paul and let you know.'

Sarah gave her a bottle of iron tablets and said goodbye. Then she sat down to write up her notes, thankful that the day was almost over. She was still getting accustomed to daylight saving, and realised that she had at least another two and a half hours of sunlight left.

Completing the work, she tidied her desk then gave her neck a massage. Sebastian would be champing at the bit, waiting impatiently for her to ride him. But before she could look forward to that she must see if Ren's hire car had arrived. Hopefully, he had reconsidered his decision to stay.

She tracked him down in the lounge room, lying on the couch with an open book on his chest, his breathing deep as he slept. Sarah slipped quietly into an armchair, taking the opportunity to study him unmasked.

His face held strong character lines that proved he'd been a student of a multitude of experiences. There was a slight sadness about his eyes and Sarah wondered what had caused it. She remembered the vulnerability last night when he'd spoken about people, loving and caring. Was there anyone special in his life? She didn't think so, mainly because he seemed the type of person who was always on the go—much like herself.

If he did have any romantic attachments they couldn't be serious. After all, he *had* made a few passes at her. She recalled all too easily what his hands had felt like against her waist when she'd backed into him the other day. They were warm and soft, yet held her in place.

She looked at his lips and knew, instinctively, that they would be soft and gentle, as well as masterful and persuasive. She licked her own in anticipation of one day tasting those lips.

'My sentiments exactly,' Ren drawled, and Sarah's eyes snapped up to meet his. They held a twinkle of laughter and a lot of desire. He levered himself up into a sitting position and leaned forward, placing his elbows on his knees.

He studied her intently for a few seconds, before reaching forward and capturing her chin in his palm. They were now only millimetres apart and Sarah closed her eyes, waiting—longing for their union. Deep down inside, she knew that it had been inevitable from the moment she'd laid eyes on him.

His lips were as soft and gentle as she'd hoped. Liquid fire coursed through her body, bringing it to life. She wanted Ren to deepen the kiss, to take her in his arms, to hold her close to his heart as though he would never let her go. Instead he gave her a few more sensual kisses, before pulling away.

He captured her gaze and ran his thumb lightly over the area his mouth had just covered. 'You're stunning,' he whispered, before lowering his head to repeat his earlier actions.

The shrill of the phone interrupted them and they broke apart instantly, years of medical training having taught them to stop whatever they were doing and answer the persistent ringing.

Sarah jumped up and raced into the kitchen, unsure of how her wobbly legs had carried her there.

'Dr Rutherford.'

'Hi. This is Toni from TransHire. Is Ren there, please?'

Sarah cleared her throat. Did this mean that he was leaving? And, more to the point, did she want him to?

'Sure, I'll get him for you,' Sarah spoke into the receiver and turned to call Ren, only to find that she didn't need to. He had followed her into the kitchen and was lounging in the doorway.

'It's the about the hire car,' she said, unable to meet his eyes. He took the receiver from her and Sarah made a dash for her bedroom, but not before she'd heard him say in a jovial tone, 'Toni. Wonderful to hear your lovely voice again.'

Quietly but firmly closing her bedroom door, Sarah threw herself down onto her bed. She was so mixed up, so confused. She didn't deny that she had wanted Ren to kiss her. Didn't deny that she'd enjoyed it. But the man was infuriating. He made her blood boil. Whether it was with anger, frustration, impatience or passion. It didn't matter. The fact was that Ren Taylor had a hold over her. He made her *feel* things she didn't want to feel. He made her rebel with an urge she hadn't felt since her father had sent her to boarding school.

There was a knock on her door and Sarah quickly crossed the room to open it. She half hid herself behind it in the hope that this might give her protection from whatever it was he was about to say.

Ren stood in the hallway and Sarah briefly saw his eyes flutter down to her lips for a moment, before returning to look at her. 'I've cancelled the hire car.' His voice reverberated through her body, the words echoing in her head. 'I've decided to stay.'

CHAPTER FOUR

ONCE they'd crossed the last paddock and Sarah had closed the gate behind her, Sebastian took off at a gallop. She let the cool evening breeze flow around her, thankful for its calming affect.

Ren Taylor was going to be her undoing. Why on earth had she let him kiss her? Although she had fantasised about him holding her, kissing her and making her lose control with the desire and passion that flooded through her when he was around it didn't mean that she had to follow it through.

Admitting that she was attracted to him was only half her battle, she realised. Attraction wasn't everything— but it's a good place to start, a little voice in her head spoke out. Sarah focused her attention on her riding technique, banishing all thoughts of Ren from her mind.

Twenty minutes later, with a healthy, rosy glow in her cheeks, Sarah dismounted outside Edith's home and led Sebastian over to the stables to have a drink.

'Hello, missy,' Trevor said as he sauntered in, Bluey at his heels. 'You're a bit late this evening. Did your clinic run overtime?'

'No,' Sarah sighed and bent to stroke her dog. 'It's just been a hectic day.'

Trevor chuckled. 'Keeping you on your toes, is he?'

'Who?' Sarah asked, feigning ignorance.

'Ren Taylor—that's who.' Trevor came and put a hand on her shoulder. 'Why don't you go on up to the house and have a good woman-to-woman chat with Edith. I'll look after Sebastian.'

Sarah reached up and kissed his cheek. 'Thanks,' she said, before departing. She found Edith sitting at the kitchen table, drinking tea, a cup already laid out for a guest.

'Expecting someone?' Sarah asked as she came through the door.

'Only you. Sit down and tell me what's wrong.'

Sarah shook her head and smiled. 'How do you do it? Are you an empath?'

'No, missy. Not at all. Ren called here. Said you'd gone storming out of the house and slammed the back door without so much as a word. He sounded worried about you. Have you two had a fight?'

Sarah fumed at his audacity, then realised that she was under very close scrutiny and slumped her arms and head onto the table. 'I don't know what's happening,' she wailed. She lifted her head and looked the older woman in the eye. 'Edith, I'm so confused.'

'He makes you feel things about yourself that you don't want to feel, doesn't he?'

Sarah nodded. 'But it's more than that. He infuriates me. I know I've got a bad temper.' She picked up her tea and took a sip, ignoring Edith's snort of agreement. 'And you must admit that I've learned to control it a lot better since I came back from overseas.'

'That you have.'

'Well, I seem to be losing my temper constantly with Ren. He seems to have burst into my life and taken over. He's now announced—not asked, but announced—that he's going to stay here for the next few weeks. He says he has holiday time owing to him and that he couldn't think of a better place to rest and relax than here. And guess where he's decided to stay? At my house,' Sarah answered, not giving Edith the slightest bit of time to guess.

'I mean, the town is already abuzz with gossip about the two of us. I think half the patients only came to the clinic today, hoping to get a glimpse of him. I've had a plethora of people ask me about him, their eyebrows raised in eagerness to hear what I've had to say.'

'And what did you say?' Edith asked calmly, and Sarah realised that her voice had risen.

'That he's a colleague from Hobart,' she said with a resigned sigh.

'Well, isn't he?'

'I guess so, but I hardly know him.' She spread her arms out wide as if to emphasise her point.

'Then get to know him. He's giving you two weeks. Talk to him, Sarah, find out what he's really like. You've always been too afraid to trust people because of your own bad experiences. And, in the meantime, let him help you with your practice if he wishes. If he's going to stay make him earn his keep. Let him run a clinic or see some patients and take the afternoon off. Enjoy yourself—go for a long ride on Sebastian or drive to Hobart to see some of your old friends. It's only a few hours' drive and you know what they say— a change is as good as a holiday!'

'Maybe,' Sarah replied with a nonchalant shrug. 'He just makes me feel so. . . Oh, I don't know.'

'Out of your depth? What's the expression they use nowadays?' Edith tapped her finger to her chin. 'Out of your comfort zone. That's it. Ren is making you step outside your comfort zone.'

'Yes, but where am I stepping? Out of the frying-pan into the fire? Half the time I feel as though I'm teetering on the edge of a cliff. You know, like when you dream that you're falling—that's how I feel.' Sarah pushed her cup aside and buried her head in her hands.

She was quiet for a moment, before glancing up to look at Edith. 'You can wipe that silly grin right off your face, Edith Ross. I don't mean falling in *that* sense of the word.'

'But you do find him attractive, don't you? How can you not? I think he's absolutely gorgeous, and so do half the women in town who've had the privilege of meeting him.'

Sarah shook her head. 'He does seem to have woven a spell around the people of this town. Even Bertie took a shine to him—if you could imagine Bertie taking a shine to anyone, that is.'

Edith chuckled. 'How was she today?'

Sarah, relieved to have the topic of conversation turned away from such personal matters, related the latest on Bertie—as well as Lizzie. 'Do you think you can organise a meal roster for the Dumars, at least for the next two weeks? I know Lizzie's mother is due to arrive at the end of this week but, until then, the more support the townsfolk can give her the better.'

'Say no more, dear.' Edith reached over to pat her hand. 'I'll get on to it right away.'

'Thanks.' Sarah stood and took their cups to the sink. After washing them, she glanced at her watch. 'I'd better be going. Is there anything I need to take home with me?'

'No, missy.' Edith stood and embraced her. 'Trevor's already taken your meal over. No doubt Ren has it all prepared and waiting on the table for you. Off you go before it gets any darker.'

'Thanks again. . .for everything.'

When she reached her own stables Sarah brushed Sebastian down and prepared his feed, talking softly to him. She was in a much better frame of mind when she opened the back door and walked through to the kitchen than when she'd left.

Contrary to Edith's usual insight, the food was not spread out, with an irresistible Ren waiting for her. It was on the bench, waiting to be reheated. She took care of the necessary preparations before going for a walk through the rest of the house.

Ren wasn't around. The door to his bedroom was closed and Sarah hesitantly knocked. She waited for a reply and when none came she gently opened the door. His belongings were still neatly placed around the room but there was no sign of him.

Feeling weary, Sarah had a quick shower before she sat down at the kitchen table to eat. Strangely enough, for the first time in a long time she felt lonely.

The shrill of the phone was a welcome interruption to Sarah's tossing and turning. She looked at the clock— almost four in the morning. Untangling herself from the bedclothes, she flung open her door and raced toward the kitchen.

'Dr Rutherford,' she answered, her voice holding no traces of sleep.

'Doc, it's Ruby. She's not well. She wasn't feeling well earlier and didn't want me to call you, but she's been vomiting, Doc, and I'm really worried about her.'

'Just as well you did call, Bill.' Sarah projected her best doctor's voice down the line, hoping to give Bill the reassurance he was searching for. 'How many times has she been sick?'

'Three. It's our fortieth wedding anniversary and

she cooked a marvellous meal, Doc.'

'I'm sure she did. Is she conscious?'

'Yes, but very tired. She's sweating and shivering at the same time.'

'I need to examine her, Bill, so I'll come right over. Bye.' Sarah hung up the phone and turned to see Ren, standing in the doorway.

'Problems?' he asked in that deep voice of his that made her quiver from top to toe.

'Ruby Maddox,' she said, after giving his body the once-over. He was fully dressed in jeans and shirt, and even had his boots on. 'Gallstones. I've tried her on a course of antibiotics and she was due to see me in the clinic on Thursday.' Sarah brushed passed him, trying to calm her finely attuned senses as their bodies touched, and made her way to her consulting room. Ren followed, hot on her heels.

'Her husband's just called to say that she's been vomiting, sweating and shivering.'

'How old is she?'

'Sixty-one, although her husband's at least ten years her senior.'

'Do you need to do a cholecystectomy?' he asked quietly as Sarah continued to throw things into her doctor's bag.

'Looks that way.' She ran a hand through her hair and looked him in the eye. 'I'm going to need your help, Ren.'

He nodded and she continued, 'Her husband, Bill, is too fragile himself to carry her anywhere so we need to get her back here, operate and then arrange for Trevor to transfer them to Hobart when she's stabilised.' Sarah glanced around her office, mentally ticking things off in her mind. She called Kate and then Ed, her anaesthetist, informing them of the situation.

'We're leaving now to collect her. I'll leave the house open so you and Kate can get started on the prep-arations.'

'Right you are, Sarah,' Ed agreed.

'OK.' She replaced the receiver and reached for her keys and bag. 'I think that's all. Let's go.'

'Aren't you forgetting one little thing, Sarah?' Ren asked, his eyes appraising her long, bare legs. 'Clothes. They'd probably be beneficial. . .not that I'm com-plaining,' he added.

Sarah looked down at herself. She was only wearing her usual thigh-length T-shirt. She grinned at Ren. 'Just as well you were here to point out that small fact.' He stood back from the door to let her pass.

'I'll put your bag in the car and wait for you,' he said as she shut her bedroom door and reached for her jeans.

Seven minutes later they pulled up outside the Maddoxes' home and raced inside. Ruby was lying on the bed, sweating and moaning although she was wear-ing only a cotton nightie.

'Ruby?' Sarah said firmly. 'Show me exactly where you hurt.'

'Here,' she whispered, and pointed to the lower part of her ribs on the right side of her body.

'She's very pale, isn't she, Doc?' Bill, dressed in his pyjamas with a robe secured around them, asked from the doorway, wringing his hands together in anxiety.

'Yes, she is, Bill,' Sarah replied as she reached into her bag and withdrew a small vial and syringe. 'I'm just going to give her something for the pain. We need to operate tonight, Ruby,' Sarah said gently. 'Is that all right with you?'

'Yes. Help me. . .please?' Ruby said through the pain.

'Is it her gallstones?' Bill asked, his voice shaking more than it had done previously.

'Yes. Dr Taylor and I will remove her gall bladder because if we don't it may rupture and then Ruby would be very ill.' She swabbed and administered the injection. Within a few seconds Ruby's face relaxed slightly and Sarah turned to face her husband.

'She needs you to be strong for her, Bill.' Sarah walked over and put her arm on his shoulder. 'This operation will make her better and it's not a complicated one at all. In fact. . .' she looked up as Ren entered the room '. . .it's just as well Dr Taylor is here with us as he's a surgeon. So she'll have two fantastic doctors looking after her.' Sarah smiled and hoped that the reassurance would help.

'I've prepared the car so we're all ready to move Ruby,' Ren said with authority.

'I'm coming too,' Bill said urgently.

'Of course you are. We wouldn't leave you behind,' Sarah said gently. 'So pull on some outdoor clothes and lock up the house. We'll meet you at the car.' Once Bill had left Ren and Sarah manoeuvred Ruby onto the portable stretcher and carried her to the four-wheel-drive.

'I'll need to call Edith once we get home. Bill can't be left on his own while we're operating,' Sarah said softly, and Ren agreed. Just as they'd finished securing Ruby, Bill appeared and they were on their way.

Bill sat in the front with Ren and gave him directions while Sarah monitored Ruby's condition.

'If you go around to the back of the house it will be easier to transfer Ruby inside,' Sarah said quietly as Ren turned into her driveway.

They carried her inside and transferred her to the barouche. Kate and Ed were almost finished with their preparations and Sarah quickly put the call through to Edith, explaining that they were about to scrub.

'Don't you worry about a thing, missy. When do you want to transfer her to Hobart?' Edith asked.

'Once she's stabilised, which will be after the sun is up.' She rang off and went to the preparation area, joining Ren at the scrub sink.

'Do you want me to operate? After all, I'm an ortho-paedic surgeon—not a general surgeon.'

'It still means you've had more cutting experience than I have,' she said and grinned at him. For the first time in what seemed like ages Ren smiled back at her. 'And I mean that in the nicest possible way,' she said sweetly.

'Sure you do,' he bantered, then took a deep breath. 'Let's get this nasty gall bladder out.'

Once they'd removed the gall bladder Ren examined it thoroughly and declared it to be completely intact.

'Whew!' Sarah raised her eyebrows. 'From the way she looked earlier I thought we might be dealing with a case of peritonitis.'

Ren sutured Ruby up and gave Ed permission to reverse the anaesthetic. There'd been hardly a grumble out of Kate as they'd operated and Sarah was thankful for small mercies.

'Where will you put her until she stabilises?' he asked as they peeled off their theatre garb.

'In my room. I'll quickly change the sheets before we move her. Then I'll help Kate put the theatre back to rights. Would you mind assisting Ed with the post-op checks?'

'Not at all.' He turned to look at her. 'You'd usually use the spare room, wouldn't you?'

'Usually,' she replied, unable to meet his gaze. Here was her opportunity to point out that, due to his bull-headedness, she would have to vacate her own room because he had moved in and taken over the other one. But she couldn't. He'd been in her life for two days and three nights and already it seemed as though he belonged—permanently.

'Then please do so. You must be tired, Sarah. I could hear you tossing about restlessly until the phone rang.'

'Well, if you could hear me, that would mean that you weren't sleeping either. Therefore we're both as tired as each other.' She washed her hands and child-ishly flicked the water off her fingers at him. 'This time I won't let you dominate me. Ruby goes into my room and that's final.'

Ren shrugged. 'Whatever you say.' He leaned closer to her and for a moment she thought he was going to kiss her again, but to her disappointment he simply asked, 'Do you think Edith would have made something to eat? I'm starving.'

Sarah couldn't help but laugh. 'Knowing Edith, I'd say you might be in luck.'

Ren reached for her hand. 'Well, what are we waiting for?' And he dragged her off to the kitchen.

Both Trevor and Edith had come across to keep Bill company. Trevor and Bill sat at the kitchen table, where Ren joined them, while Edith was busy in the kitchen. Sarah gave all three of them the report on Ruby's progress.

'I'll change my sheets and put her in my room where

I can monitor her. Once she's stabilised I'll arrange for her to be transferred down to Hobart. She'll need to rest and, because of her age, I'd prefer she was in hospital,' Sarah explained, her voice brooking no argument when it looked as though Bill was about to complain.

'I can go with her, can't I?' he asked hesitantly.

'Of course you can, Bill. No one's trying to keep you out of the picture—quite the opposite. Ruby's going to need you there with her. Is there anyone you can stay with?

'Our eldest son lives there.'

'Good.' Sarah nodded. 'I'll get Ruby settled, then we can make any other arrangements for you.'

'Do you want a hand, changing those sheets?' Edith asked.

'No. I think it best if you feed poor Dr Taylor.' Her eyes met with his. 'He's apparently *starving*.' Sarah stressed the word and winked at him before leaving the room.

Ruby was transferred to Sarah's room, and by eight-thirty Sarah pronounced that she was satisfied with her patient's post-operative progress. Ren had phoned through to the Royal Hobart Hospital and arranged a bed for Ruby while Sarah had organised Bill.

Trevor had the plane ready and, with Ren promising to see Lizzie Dumar on her behalf, Sarah went with her patient. By ten-thirty that morning Sarah and Trevor were sitting in her favourite café in Salamanca Place, enjoying a hot cappuccino and delicious, mouth-watering pastries.

'Mmm,' Sarah said as she took another bite of her freshly baked apricot Danish. 'This is the one place in Hobart that I've really missed.' She grinned across the table at Trevor, who was also devouring a sinful pastry.

'I used to come here every day, either for breakfast, lunch or dinner—regardless of my shift—and I used to sit at this very table every single time.' She took another bite. 'This is heaven.'

'Don't you dare tell Edith I've been eating these things,' Trevor said as he licked his fingers.

Sarah laughed. 'She'd skin us both alive if she knew. Don't worry, Trevor. This will definitely be our little secret.'

Trevor drained his cup. 'Well, that caffeine should keep us awake for the trip home. Come on, missy. We'd better be on our way.'

They took a taxi to the airport as the ambulance had brought them in. Sarah looked out of the window and felt happy but very tired. Trevor was a competent pilot and before she knew it they were landing on the small airstrip at the rear of the property.

Ren had driven her four-wheel-drive out to meet the plane and took them back to Edith's for lunch.

'Everything go smoothly?' Edith asked once they were all seated around her kitchen table.

'Just dandy,' Sarah replied, and eyed the mountain of food Edith was about to dish up onto her plate. 'Ah, I'm not all that hungry, Edith. Could you halve that amount?'

'You feeling all right, missy?' she quizzed and Sarah yawned.

'Fine. Just tired.' She tried to stop a small tell-tale blush from creeping into her cheeks. She was tired— she hadn't lied—but those pastries had been more than adequate when it came to filling the stomach. Edith relented with her inquisition and did as Sarah asked.

Trevor, on the other hand, wasn't so fortunate and

had to eat the entire portion his wife placed before him.
Oh, well, she thought with a wry chuckle, he was a
growing man.

Ren, who was seated next to her, leaned across and
whispered in her ear, 'What's so funny?'

'I'll tell you later,' she whispered back, not wanting
to get caught by Edith.

Once the meal had been eaten and lavishly praised
Ren was instructed by the woman who seemed to be
running all their lives to take Sarah home and put her
to bed.

'She works too hard and needs her rest. Especially
after she's been down to Hobart and back and it's only
just gone two o'clock.'

On the short drive back to her house Sarah asked
after Lizzie and the morning's events.

'She's fine,' he reported. 'Little Reuben didn't give
her such a hard time last night and she was showered
and dressed when I arrived, even though I was an hour
or so later than we had been yesterday.

'It was her husband, John, who was bothering me.
He seems to take it for granted that Lizzie can cope,
and that he doesn't have to lift a finger or do anything
differently from his normal routine.'

'A lot of country men are like that.'

'The older men, I can understand, but he's younger
than me. The fact remains that Lizzie can't cope, even
though help has been organised and a meal taken over
every day. That won't last for ever, and if John doesn't
get his act into gear Lizzie's going to drop from
exhaustion.'

Sarah sighed, knowing that Ren was right. 'But what
can I do?' she asked helplessly.

'No need to worry.' He leaned over and patted her knee. 'I've taken care of it.'

'Ren!' Sarah turned to face him as he brought the car to a halt outside her back door. 'What did you do?'

'After I'd seen Lizzie, I sought John out and had a few choice words with him.'

'You didn't.' Sarah didn't know whether to be pleased or offended.

'I did. The way I see it, Sarah, it's best if it came from me anyway. I'm an outsider, a doctor and I'm also a man. If you'd said anything he'd have brushed your words aside the same way he brushes his wife aside.'

'He's not that bad,' she said defensively.

'Probably not, but hopefully I've given him a few things to think about. Over the next few days we should see a happier Lizzie when we do her postnatal visits.'

Sarah laughed and shook her head. 'You're amazing, do you know that?'

'It has been mentioned before,' he replied with a smug smile.

'I'll just bet it has.' She jumped down from the car and made her way inside. She sat down at the kitchen table and yawned. Stretching languorously, she noted that Ren's attention was completely captivated by her body. Too tired to make an issue of it, she let him look. She was delighted that he found her attractive but was still unsure what to do about it.

He cleared his throat and turned his back to her. Filling the kettle, he asked, 'Do you have a clinic this afternoon?'

'No. Tuesday is usually my day to catch up, but at the moment I'm too tired to do any paperwork.'

He nodded. 'Then you can tell me what you were chuckling over at lunch.'

Sarah smiled again. 'So long as you promise not to tell Edith.'

Ren made the cross-my-heart gesture which she accepted. 'Trevor and I stopped in Salamanca Place for a little coffee and cake—or rather pastry. So, by the time we got back here, neither of us were very hungry but Trevor still had to eat the entire amount of food his wife dished up for him.'

Ren grinned. 'It wasn't that café halfway down the street, hmm. . . Café Lella, isn't it?'

'That's the one. I used to eat there every day when I was working in Hobart. It's so close to the hospital.'

'I know the one. I've eaten there quite a few times myself. So, why didn't you bring me back an offering?' he said with mock severity. 'After all, I've been running around seeing your patients.'

'True, and I want you to know that I do appreciate your help.'

'That's a turn-up for the books,' he replied sardonically, and she poked her tongue out at him.

'You don't deserve any pastries after that remark,' she told him, turning on her heel and walking out of the room. He caught up with her just before she opened her bedroom door.

'I haven't changed your sheets yet,' he said, grasping both of her hands and pulling her in the direction of his own room. 'Once you'd left Edith told me she had some people to see and so I offered to take care of changing your sheets. When I'd returned from my little tête-à-tête with the Dumars she called to say you were due back any minute and could I pick you up from the airstrip? So,' he continued, 'why don't you rest on my bed? After all, my orders were to bring you back here and put you to bed.'

'I couldn't do that. It won't take me long to rechange the sheets. Besides, where will you sleep?'

'I'm not that tired.'

'Liar. You've been up as long as I have. . .longer probably.' Strangely enough, she let him usher her into his room and lay her down on one side of the double bed. She *was* tired and didn't feel like arguing. This would be one time when she'd let him take charge, she promised herself as he knelt and removed her boots, before doing the same with his own.

Sarah watched as he lay down next to her. He must have read the wide-eyed panic displayed across her face because he said, 'Don't worry, Sarah. I'm not going to ravish you. I'm much too tired. Just lie here and sleep beside me. . .please?' He gathered her into his arms before she had a chance to protest.

She laid her head on his chest and listened to the soothing sound of his heartbeat. It was completely innocent, she told herself. They were both fully clothed, above the covers and extremely tired.

She relaxed a little further as she felt his fingers flow gently through her hair.

'Ren. . .' she said sleepily.

'Shh,' he replied, and tightened his hold. 'Go to sleep, Sarah.'

She closed her heavy eyelids and snuggled closer to him. He felt so wonderful and Sarah realised how right it was for her to be in his arms. Her last thought before she drifted off into a deep sleep was that she was glad she'd bought a kettle that switched off automatically.

CHAPTER FIVE

SARAH raised her arms above her head and stretched her body. Letting out a deep breath, she rubbed her eyes. What a fantastic sleep! Her whole body felt relaxed, revitalised and raring to go. She swung her legs over the side of the bed and stretched again before her eyes focused on her surroundings.

This wasn't her room—this was the spare room. . . correction. . .Ren's room! She turned and checked the bed, thankful that he wasn't in it.

'I'd better get out of here,' she mumbled and made her way to the door—collecting her boots in the process. She made no noise as she slipped quickly into her own room and leant against the closed door, her heart hammering in her ears.

'Nothing happened,' she told herself as she recalled exactly how she'd ended up in Ren's room. Sarah raised a hand to her cheeks—they felt hot. She dared a glance in her mirror and had her suspicions confirmed. She was blushing because even though nothing *had* happened she had wanted it to. How on earth was she going to face him again without this tell-tale blush?

She remembered the feeling of completion as Ren had held her securely in his arms, his soothing fingers running through her hair—causing her to fall into a deep and therapeutic sleep.

'Sarah,' she told her reflection, 'get a grip on yourself. Ren Taylor is not the kind of man you want to fall in love with. He's arrogant, overbearing. . .' She listed the adjectives that, as far as she was concerned, had become synonymous with his name. 'And he's just not right for you.' She nodded for emphasis but her reflection looked as though it didn't really believe her.

A shower—that was what she needed, and a cold one at that. She gathered her things together and crept along the hallway to the bathroom. Thankfully the door was open, which meant that Ren had to be somewhere else around the house.

Sarah washed away the cares of her long day and noticed, as she was towelling herself dry, that it was dark outside the bathroom window. She guess it to be around eight-thirty and received an answering growl from her stomach which confirmed her thoughts.

Feeling refreshed from her shower, Sarah dressed and followed the delicious aroma that her nose had discovered. It led her into the kitchen and her eyes witnessed Ren, standing at the stove and stirring a pot.

'Mmm. What smells so yummy?' she asked, her previous apprehension regarding Ren disappearing in the light of feeding herself.

'Spaghetti sauce,' he answered, turning when he heard her voice. His eyes travelled the length of her, dressed comfortably and casually in a fresh pair of denims and a bright red T-shirt. His appraisal caused her heart to leap into her throat and she quickly swallowed, trying to quell the sensation.

'Is Edith spoiling you again with pasta?' she queried as she walked over to the stove—her eyes fixed on the pots rather than Ren.

'Yes.'

Sarah could feel his eyes assessing her and couldn't resist the tug that forced her head up to meet his gaze.

'Spaghetti Bolognese is another favourite of mine—

among other things,' he said softly. They almost were standing toe to toe but if she raised herself up slightly and leaned closer Sarah was positive that their lips would touch.

She was still deciding whether this would be a wise move when Ren took the decision out of her hands and bent his head to claim her lips. They were all that she'd remembered, and more.

This time his kiss was more of an exploration as he nibbled and suckled at her lips before his probing tongue sought entrance to her mouth. His hands slid up her arms, drawing her closer to him. Sarah felt wave after wave of bliss flow over her at the sensations he was evoking.

She glided her palms up over his chest, relishing the feel of his muscled torso beneath his cotton shirt, before they continued their journey around to his back. Ren gathered her closer to him, their bodies now aligned with each other—the kiss deepening further.

His mouth was now hot and demanding on hers and Sarah felt herself getting swept away with the passion. She was pliant in his arms and loving it. It didn't matter what angry or emotional words had passed between them before—this was what she wanted, where she wanted to be.

His mouth left hers, temporarily, to trail small butterfly kisses down her neck and Sarah breathed in deeply, drowning in his pure masculine scent. This was bliss, as far as she was concerned, and all she wanted now was for their passion to take its natural course.

Ren slowly drew his lips away from hers, kissing the tip of her nose, her eyes and her forehead before tucking her securely against his chest. Their breathing was hectic but was beginning to steady as they held each other tight.

Why had he stopped? Had she done something wrong? Sarah felt bewildered and slightly miffed that he'd ended the most sensual feeling she'd ever felt. Slowly she raised her head and looked into his eyes.

He must have read her confusion because he bent and placed a quick kiss on her now—swollen lips before releasing her from his embrace.

'The spaghetti should be ready now,' he said, his voice completely normal and under control. He turned from her and gave the pot one last stir before he checked the pasta that was bubbling on the back burner.

'The spaghetti can fizzle and dry up, for all I care,' Sarah blurted out. 'What about us? What about everything we just experienced—what we shared?' She balled her hands into fists as Ren drained the pasta and began serving onto the plates.

When a few seconds had ticked by and it appeared to Sarah that he was planning to ignore her she stepped forward and turned him to face her.

'Answer me, Ren. You know it infuriates me even further when you play your little ignoring games. Why did you stop?'

He took a deep breath and looked longingly into her eyes. 'Because you would have despised me even more if I'd swept you up and carried you off to one of the bedrooms.'

'So?' Her fuzzy brain tried to rationalise. 'I thought you wanted me? You certainly gave me that impression yesterday afternoon when you kissed me. What's changed your mind, Ren? Have you decided that I don't measure up to your standards after all?'

'Not at all. Sarah. . .' He reached for her but she

eluded him. Her eyes were blazing with anger, her lips were red from his kisses, and he thought she'd never looked more beautiful.

'It's true.' He dropped his hands back to his side and lazily hooked a thumb through his jeans pockets. 'I do want you and if this had happened yesterday I probably would have carried you off and made love to you. . .'

'But,' she said, feeling her anger beginning to diminish but still wanting to stay mad at him.

'But things have changed within the last twenty-four hours. I want us to get to know each other—not just be ships in the night.'

He'd clearly surprised her as Sarah felt her mouth fall open. Of all the things she'd been expecting him to say that wasn't one of them.

'What I'd like to suggest is that we sit down and eat this wonderful meal, then go for a walk. Let's talk, Sarah. Build a foundation.'

'A foundation for what?'

He shrugged. 'I'm not sure yet. Can't we at least try to see if there is something other than fantastic passion between us?'

Sarah thought long and hard for at least one whole minute, before nodding her head in agreement. 'OK. Let's give it a try but, as far as I'm concerned, honesty must be the basis of any foundation.'

'My sentiments exactly. Now can we please eat?' he said and treated her to one of his heart-warming smiles. She smiled back.

'Certainly. I'll set the table.'

Ren was charming and entertaining while they ate, making Sarah feel comfortable with their new truce. Their discussion was centred on general medical issues

and the different advances in the medical field during
the past twenty years.

They cleared the table and stacked the dishwasher
before Sarah checked the weather outside. Although the
evenings could still get quite cool she decided that she
didn't need a jumper for her walk with Ren.

She clipped her mobile phone to the waistband of
her jeans and shrugged as Ren saw her do so. 'When
you're the only doctor for miles you're always on call.'

The moon, although not full, provided them with
sufficient light so that a torch wasn't necessary. Besides,
Sarah could find her way around the property blind-
folded.

'Does it bother you to be on call twenty-four hours
a day, seven days a week, every week of the year?'
Ren asked as he reached out for her hand. Sarah waited
for the tingling sensation his touch evoked to settle
down before she trusted her voice enough to
answer him.

'Sometimes. Although I seem to have months when
it's extremely busy and then three to four months at a
stretch where only minor ailments are the flavour and
they can be dealt with during the clinics.'

'How many do you have per week?'

'Two big clinics and two small clinics. As I said,
Tuesday is my only day with no clinics and I sometimes
feel as though I'm living from one Tuesday to the next.
The community are very receptive to the hours I've
outlined and unless it's an emergency they'll leave it
until Wednesday to see me.'

'How do you differentiate between a big clinic and
a small clinic?' he asked, and Sarah realised that he was
really interested—he wasn't just making conversation.

'The hours. Monday afternoon's clinic goes from two

until six and Wednesday's from three until five. Thursday is my big day and that's from ten in the morning until five that afternoon. That's usually when the folk from the surrounding communities book in for their check-ups; and then Friday afternoons from three until five.

'As I said, they're the times I've outlined that I'm available for clinics and I usually have my weekends free, except for the home visits which I do every day—but they only take a few hours.'

'Apart from Monday mornings when you go and clean Bertie's house. You do too much, Sarah. Another doctor is needed for this area or at least a district nurse. Why don't you apply to the government for one?'

'Don't flog a dead horse, Ren,' she said, using his turn of phrase. 'Besides, not many people want to come out here. The money isn't that good and the only reason I'm here is because this is my home, my community.'

'Do you feel that you owe it to them?' His questions were asked in a calm and logical manner but Sarah could feel the urgency running through his words.

'Not really, but the fact remains that if there had been a regular general practitioner in this district instead of a rotation of doctors coming from either Hobart or Launceston to do clinics then maybe my father's viral pleurisy would have been diagnosed and treated earlier than it was.'

'Sarah.' Ren stopped walking and turned her to face him. 'Surely you don't blame yourself for your father's death?'

'If I had come back here to work after completing my internship in Hobart instead of running away overseas for five years then, yes, maybe he still would be alive today.' She walked on ahead, not wanting to face

Ren as she dredged up the painful memories. 'Oh, I know he didn't hold it against me. In fact, in the last months of his life we became closer than we ever had.'

They started walking again and for a while neither of them spoke—each lost in their own thoughts.

'I was an only child as well,' Ren said softly as he reached for her hand. 'My parents are the epitome of English aristocracy. Sir William—the famous QC.' His tone had turned bitter and Sarah gave his hand a little squeeze of sympathy. 'As such, he and my mother had absolutely nothing to do with my upbringing—except to pay someone else to do it. I've been in this country now for almost twelve years and have not the slightest intention of ever seeing them again.'

'You don't have to talk about it if you don't want to. There are other ways we can get to know each other, without giving a running history of our lives.'

'Such as?' he queried, his voice returning to normal.

'What's your favourite colour?' Sarah asked lightly.

'What?'

'You heard me—what's your favourite colour?'

He seemed to be thinking about it, as though he'd never even thought of liking one specific colour above others. 'Burgundy. What's yours?'

'The only way to describe it is a dark navy blue. Like the sky on a cloudless yet starry night.' They both looked up at the sky, then laughed. 'Next question,' Sarah announced. 'What kind of music do you like listening to?'

'Gilbert and Sullivan,' he announced without thought. 'And you?'

Sarah chuckled. 'Nothing remotely G and S, although I don't mind them. I like Billy Joel.'

Ren nodded. 'My turn to ask a question.' They'd

arrived at the long wooden fence that took them into the next paddock and Sarah leaned her arms on the top railing, edging her foot onto a lower rung. 'Your favourite food?'

'Hey, that's not a fair question because I already know what your favourite food is. Any type of pasta— *and* I've had to endure it.'

He laughed but didn't concede the point. 'Favourite food, please?'

'OK,' she relented. 'Chocolate-covered strawberries, but I get to ask you an extra question.' He didn't refuse so Sarah asked, 'What's something you really like doing—what relaxes you?'

His face was all dark angles and Sarah couldn't read his expression at all, but his voice was almost husky when he answered. 'I like to be fussed.'

Sarah's eyes widened. 'Dare I ask what exactly that entails?'

'It's when someone does this. . .' Ren gathered her closely into his arms and rested her head on his chest. He began to run his fingers through Sarah's hair, just as he had done earlier in the day. 'This is what I term to be "a fuss". One of my favourite nannies used to put me to sleep this way when I was a child. It would unwind me, help me sleep. It helped me to realise that someone in the world did love me, even if that person was paid by my parents to care for my daily needs.'

Sarah sighed against his chest. She knew exactly what he was talking about, not to mention the sensations he was once again bringing to life with his so-called 'fuss'. It did relax her. It did make her feel loved and needed. Just like she loved and needed him.

She buried her head deeper into his chest, her arms reaching around to hold him closer. The realisation of

the true emotions she felt for Ren had hit her like a ton
of bricks and she knew she was blushing.

They stood like that for at least another ten minutes
before Ren eased Sarah away from him. He gazed down
at her and cupped her face within his large hands.
Slowly his head began its descent to claim her lips and
Sarah stood on tiptoe to assist in the process.

The kiss was powerful and passionate yet delicate.
He sensuously brushed his lips over hers, whetting her
appetite for more. She tried to capture his head, to hold
it firmly in place, but he gently eased back.

'This doesn't help in getting to know each other
better. We've already agreed that we're compatible in
this field of a relationship.'

Relationship? Sarah's heart did a flip at his words.
Did this mean that Ren thought of her as more than
just a short-term acquaintance? She began to tremble
and he mistook it for the cold.

'We'd better head back to the house. Wouldn't do
for the doctor to catch a cold.' She heard the light-
hearted teasing in his voice.

They walked in a companionable silence, their linked
hands swinging gently between them.

'Tell me some more about your time overseas—
especially the time you spent in Africa,' Ren asked after
a while.

Sarah shrugged. She usually didn't talk about her
time overseas as it brought back memories of Gregg
and the emotional turmoil he'd put her through. Thinking about it now, it didn't seem to bother her as much
as it used to so she began to tell Ren about the small,
picturesque villages she'd worked in, not only in
England but in Ireland and Scotland as well.

They reminisced about other places that they'd both

visited before she finally got around to her time in
Africa.

'The villages were almost exactly the same as you
would see on television for a commercial about world
aid, although the people were wonderful. Very
accepting, even though their cultures are so different
from ours.

'But the scenery around Zimbabwe was. . .majestic.
There's no other word to describe it. It was as though
I was standing in God's own country, His creation
surrounding me.

'Of course there were the animals which, again, are
so different. Baboons, I've decided, are the most sneaky
and cheekiest animals of all. They'd come right into
the village and steal things.' Sarah laughed out loud at
the memory.

'What kind of work did you do?' Ren queried, and
Sarah sighed.

'Just about everything. They had a witch-doctor who
would occasionally put in an appearance and, amazingly
enough, after proving myself worthy, he actually taught
me a thing or two.'

Now it was Ren's turn to laugh. 'Do the people of
this community know that you studied under a witch-
doctor? I can just see Bertie letting you perform some
ancient ritual to restore her eyesight, like putting on a
paste of baboon dung mixed with rhinoceros urine with
the added touch of saliva and an ostrich feather—just
to give it artistic impression.'

'Not rhinoceros urine,' Sarah said in a serious tone.
'Zebra urine.'

Ren pulled her to a halt. 'I was just fooling around.
You are joking, aren't you?'

Sarah couldn't resist her mirth any longer and gave

way to it. 'Yes, of course I'm joking.' They began to
walk again. 'Besides, I had to take an oath of secrecy
to protect the villagers' rights. To tell you the truth,
Ren, I don't get much of a call for witch-doctor medicine here. Although I'd never dispute the fact that it
works, it's not really my style.'

'And what about this jig—for hip operations. How
did that come about?'

Sarah glanced sideways at Ren but it was too dark
to read his expression. Ethically, she wasn't sure about
discussing it with anyone—except the old Hound—due
to the fact that it wasn't patented. Anyone could steal
her idea—you can't patent ideas.

But this is Ren, her heart told her head. He's already
said that he may be able to help you get through to the
old Hound so why not take the chance and trust him?

She knew that Ren was aware of her hesitation but
he didn't push her and she was grateful.

'There had been a tribal dispute and one of the chiefs
from a neighbouring village had been badly injured. He
had multiple lacerations that needed suturing and had
broken his hand and wrist but they were clean breaks
so I could simply plaster them. He'd also, and I'm still
not sure exactly how he did it, fractured his hip in
several places.

'My first problem was obtaining permission for him
to have a general anaesthetic, and once this had been
done my nurse and I began surgery. The top of the
hip-bone was almost shattered and I needed an instrument that would let me stabilise parts of the bone and
hold it firmly in place before I could continue with the
next section.

'My instruments were all at least five to ten years
old and very outdated, which is the main reason I have

my surgery here so well stocked. Amazingly enough, this crude instrument worked, and when I finally returned to civilisation I thought it was worth a closer look. I don't profess to be an inventor or up to date on orthopaedic inventions, which is why I want the professor to look at it and give me his opinion.' Sarah kicked the ground in frustration. 'But, obviously, he's just too busy.'

They walked in silence for a few moments before she asked quietly, 'Do you think I should forget it? I mean, you're probably up to date on the latest techniques and inventions in the hip replacement field—what's your professional opinion?'

It was Ren's turn to hesitate, before saying carefully, 'I'd need to see the prototype. When exactly are you expecting it in?'

'Not until Friday but I have got a copy of the design specifications, if that helps,' Sarah offered eagerly. Now that she'd told him she felt so much better.

'That might give me more of an idea of what it looks like. Mind if I take a look tomorrow morning?'

'Not at all.' Sarah's heart felt lighter than it had in years. Having a professional medical colleague to talk to was wonderful, and the fact that he specialised in the area that she needed help in was a bonus.

'I have one last question for you,' Ren said as they neared Sarah's back verandah. 'What made you decided to work overseas?'

Sarah smiled up at him. 'The usual—a broken heart.'

'Really? That's very. . .emotional of you, Sarah,' he teased and she laughed.

'He was all wrong for me and I now view my escape overseas as one of the best decisions I've made in my life. It gave me personal and medical experience, confidence to follow through with my convictions and opened a door to a world of different cultures and aspects of human life. I returned an enriched woman and can't thank Gregg enough for jilting me.'

'Where is he now?'

'I've no idea. Wanted to marry money and thought I had some,' Sarah said in a conspiratorial whisper.

'Foolish man,' Ren said softly as they reached the lamplight of the verandah. She looked up at him and he lowered his head for a brief and fleeting kiss. 'It was a lovely walk Sarah. Thank you.'

'My pleasure,' Sarah replied with full meaning to the words. After all it wasn't every night you discovered you were in love.

'Time for bed. You to yours and me to mine.'

'And never the twain shall meet,' Sarah joked as she climbed the back stairs into the house.

'Good morning,' Ren said, looking up from the design specifications for her prototype. Sarah had dug them out and left him at the kitchen table, pouring over them, when she'd gone to do her morning housecalls—and he was still there, drinking a cup of coffee.

'Is it still morning?' Sarah glanced at her watch. It was only just after ten o'clock but it felt as though she'd been up for hours.

Ren chuckled. 'That bad, eh? How's Lizzie and baby Reuben?'

'Both fine. Her milk's come in but Kate's been on hand to help her out in that department. John was even there this morning—cooking breakfast for his wife!' She grinned and sat down opposite him. 'Whatever you said it worked. Between having a little bit of attention from her husband, female support and the main meal of the day taken off her hands, Lizzie looks so much happier than she did a day or two ago. I must give Edith a call and thank her for organising the ladies.'

Sarah stood and poured herself some coffee—in her second-favourite coffee-cup. 'So what do you think?' she asked, pointing to the specifications in front of him.

'Not bad.' He raised his eyebrows and nodded his head to add positive emphasis to his words. 'Especially for someone who isn't an orthopod. There are a few suggestions I have but, as I said last night, I would need to see the prototype first.' He held up a hand as Sarah opened her mouth. 'I'll not say another word on the subject until then.'

'Fair enough,' Sarah sighed.

'Clinic this afternoon?' Ren asked as he watched her lean against the bench and sip her drink.

'Just a small one. I've got a lot of paperwork to catch up on that should have been completed yesterday. That is, provided the phone doesn't. . .'

Her words were too late as the telephone shrilled to life. She sighed and put her cup down, before lifting the receiver.

'Dr Rutherford.' Sarah listened to the frantic child explain about the pain her mother was in. Sarah quickly took notes, before replacing the receiver.

'It's Margaret Braithwaite. She has fibroids and it sounds as though a pedicle has twisted. I saw her in my clinic on Monday and was waiting on her decision regarding surgery.'

'Symptoms?'

'From what her eldest daughter said, she's got a lot of pain in the belly and was rolling around. Her husband's bringing her in so I'll know soon enough what's happening. I'll call Kate and Ed and have them on standby.'

Sarah walked to the door, before turning to face Ren who was almost directly behind her. 'That is, if you don't mind helping?'

Ren smiled down at her. 'Sarah, you can take it for granted that as long as I'm here you can count on my assistance. Look upon it as my way of paying board.'

She nodded and resumed her way down the hall to her consulting room. Why did he have to stand so close? Smile so irresistibly at her? It made her heart beat faster and her knees turn to jelly.

Forcing herself to concentrate on the task at hand, she sifted through her patient files to find Margaret's notes. She handed them to Ren to look at so he could familiarise himself with the case.

'So you think we should be prepared to find the worst?' Ren asked as he replaced the file on Sarah's desk.

'I think we should open the uterus and remove the offending fibroid. On the other hand, Margaret has already had six children, and if those fibroids keep playing up it may be better to do a hysterectomy—depending on the patient's opinion, of course.'

'Of course,' he reiterated. 'Do you want to take the lead?'

'You're the surgeon,' Sarah countered.

'Yes, but you're not just your average GP. With the experience you gained overseas, I'd say you've probably done a few more hysterectomies than I have.'

'Fine.' Sarah nodded her agreement. Would their working routine be as smooth, with her playing the surgeon and Ren assisting? They'd soon find out. She called Ed and Kate and was going through her mental check-list when they heard a car pull up.

Ren wheeled the barouche out onto the front verandah

and helped Paul Braithwaite carry his wife up the steps. Sarah took her pulse—it was extremely high.

'You're welcome to stay,' Sarah said to Paul, and gestured to the kitchen. 'I can't say how long we'll be as I'm not sure what we'll find.' They watched as Ren and the barouche disappeared behind the preparation doors.

'I've got the middle two kids with me so I'd better get back home to the rest of them. Call me as soon as you know anything,' Paul said, wiping sweat from his brow.

'I promise.' Sarah placed a hand on his shoulder, before turning and following Ren.

'Margaret?' Sarah waited for her patient's eyes to focus. 'I need to examine you and ask some questions.' Ren handed Sarah a chart and she noted the symptoms. The abdomen was distended, her temperature was up and she was extremely pale and sweaty.

'Margaret? We need to operate but first I must explain that, depending on what we find with regard to your fibroids, it may be better for us to perform a complete hysterectomy. Have you discussed this with Paul?'

'Yes. If you think it's necessary, Sarah. I'm not so worried about the operation any more—just the children. How long will I be in hospital?'

'About a week, but you won't be allowed to do anything physical for about six to eight weeks—like lifting or bending. The kids will help you out. Now, I need you to sign this consent form and we can begin.' Sarah re-explained the procedure before Margaret signed. Ed arrived, set up an IVT and gave pre-medication.

'That should help,' he said and smiled down at Margaret, before organising himself for the operation. Kate arrived, grumbled at all of them and began work.

Sarah shook her head in bemusement and joined Ren at the scrub sink.

When everyone was ready Sarah made the incision in the abdominal wall. She took one look at the twisted fibroid and let out a whistle. Most of the other fibroids were well on their way to the same state. 'Do you agree to a hysterectomy?' she asked Ren.

'Agreed.'

'Right. Let's get to it.' The uterus was removed and soon the operation was over.

'Time to change the sheets and organise another trip to Hobart,' Sarah said as they degowned.

'And this time—' Ren pointed his finger at her '—bring me back some yummy pastries and cakes.'

Sarah laughed and ran her fingers through her hair. 'You're on.' She called Paul Braithwaite to let him know his wife's condition, then wrote up Margaret's notes and organised her transfer.

Her clinic for that afternoon was light—only five patients were booked in. She should have no difficulty transferring them to tomorrow's clinic. She'd just picked up the phone when Ren came in, carrying two cups.

'Thought you could use this,' he said, and placed it on her desk. 'I've taken one in to Ed and the ever-grumbling Kate. You have milk—no sugar, right?'

'Right.' She smiled, replaced the telephone receiver and took a sip of her coffee.

'Have you contacted Trevor?' Ren seated himself opposite her, sipping his own.

'Not yet. I want to cancel my patients for this afternoon first. Besides, Edith should be over soon with lunch so I can do it then. At least this emergency came at a decent hour of the day.' She leaned back in her chair and relaxed.

'Is your clinic for tomorrow booked up?'

'Just about, and I always get some patients who simply turn up and are happy to wait to see me. I think they view it as a social outing. Let's go to the doctors' clinic, sit in the waiting room and catch up on all the latest gossip.'

'Why don't I do your clinic for you this afternoon?'

'No, Ren.' She shook her head to add emphasis to her words. Although she had come to know him better, not to mention the fact that she'd fallen in love with him, he still didn't seem to realise that she didn't need him to run her life. She could cope with her workload, which meant sometimes being putout.

The fact was indisputable that he'd been a marvellous help while he'd been here, and she'd especially appreciated it on the surgical side, but her patients were *her* patients. Knowing that he was offering only because he was concerned for her she made her voice a little softer, before saying, 'You've done too much already. You're supposed to be on holiday.'

'This *is* a holiday, compared to my average working day. Is there anything urgent that you should do personally for this clinic or are they basically check-ups and follow-ups?'

'All routine. I'll just make new appointments.'

'How many are booked in?'

'Five, though, again, there may be some who simply turn up.'

'No trouble at all.'

'Ren, you're not a GP,' she reminded him. The man was stubborn. He simply wouldn't take no for an answer. 'I know you want to help because you keep reiterating the fact that I work too much, but this time I'll have to decline.'

'Tell you what. . .' he leaned forward in his chair and looked at her intently '. . .make new appointments for those patients who are booked in, and if any turn up on the spur of the moment I'll take care of them.'

Sarah regarded him thoughtfully over the rim of her cup. 'OK. It's a deal.'

CHAPTER SIX

'I'VE no idea what Ren said to him, but for the past few days John's been a different man,' Lizzie said as she and Sarah enjoyed a cup of coffee next morning. 'Last night he even got up to the baby between feeds so that I could sleep.' She shook her head in amazement. 'It's wonderful.'

'I'm so glad. I saw him leaving as I pulled up so I presume he prepared breakfast again?'

'That's right. Nothing fancy, but at least I was able to settle Reuben and have a shower. I feel as though I can actually cope.'

Lizzie grinned and Sarah hesitated before saying, 'You know about the baby blues, don't you?' Lizzie nodded and Sarah continued, 'It usually affects new mothers between day three and five postnatal. You'll feel weepy, tired, cranky and a whole lot of other wonderful side-effects. You may not want to even *see* John, let alone have him help you. It's simply your hormones beginning to readjust to your non-pregnant state. It happens to every mother and is completely normal.'

'Kate's told me about it on her visits. Even though she appears reluctant, she's been a wonderful help and very supportive.'

'Yes, she's well trained and certainly knows her job. I'm glad she's been helpful.'

'And not only her. The other ladies who have come around to help have told me all about their experiences with motherhood, and it makes me feel as though I'm not alone in what I'm feeling.'

'You're not.'

'I can't wait for my mother to arrive. It's the first grandchild on my side of the family and I think his dear grandma is going to be wrapped around Reuben's little finger within a matter of minutes.'

Sarah laughed. 'I'm sure of it.'

'Speaking of children, how is Margaret doing?'

'Slowly getting better. Paul is coping well and the older children are very helpful. I should have a report waiting on my fax machine when I get home.' She looked at her watch. 'As much as I'm relaxing and enjoying our chat, we'd better proceed with your examination as I've got clinic this morning and want to drop in to see Bertie beforehand.'

'See—you do too much.' Lizzie stood and headed for the bedroom.

'So I've been told.'

'Ren says that the government should at least provide a district nurse for you, otherwise you'll push yourself until you drop.'

Sarah shook her head. 'That man sticks his nose in too much where it's not wanted.'

'So,' Lizzie said in a conspiratorial whisper, 'how are things going with him?' Sarah felt herself blush and Lizzie gave her a nudge. 'Say no more. So you think he's the one?'

'Oh, Lizzie, I don't know what to think, other than he's been a fantastic help on the surgical side. He has shown me that I do need some help, running my ever-growing practice, even if it is a district nurse. Once he leaves—' Sarah tried to keep her voice light '—I'll probably look into getting help.'

'At least he's achieved *that* goal,' Lizzie replied, grinning like a Cheshire cat, and Sarah ignored her innuendo.

'Let's get this exam done before your son wakes up,' Sarah said briskly.

'Whatever you say, Doc,' Lizzie said with a little laugh.

Reuben woke before Sarah left so she was able to give him a quick examination as well. Climbing into her car, she drove out to the MacPhail dump yard to check on Bertie's eyes. Edith had contacted Sarah to say that Bertie had reached a decision regarding the laser surgery in Hobart. Sarah hoped it was the *right* one.

''Bout time you got 'ere,' Bertie said when Sarah walked through the door and gave the elderly woman a kiss on the cheek. 'Where's ya offsider?'

'Oh,' Sarah smiled, 'so that's the only reason you wanted me to come? Hoping to see Dr Taylor again, were you?'

'Don't be ridiculous, ya silly girl,' Bertie reprimanded her, although Sarah could tell that she was pleased with the teasing. 'I'll have ya stupid operation that the whole town seems ta be pesterin' me ta have but there is a condition.'

'I thought there might be just one or two.'

'Watch ya mouth, girlie. If it weren't for ya father, I'd never tolerate ya interference,' Bertie admonished.

'What's the condition?' Sarah said, trying not to laugh.

'I want ya ta be there when they're doin' the operation.' She folded her arms across her chest, indicating that she would brook no argument.

'Of course I will. I've told you before, Bertie. It's

only day surgery and they'll give you a local anaesthetic, which means that you will be awake.'

'I don't wanna be awake. Also, I don't like that fella
ya sent me to.'

'Dr Branigan? What's wrong with him?'

'I just don't like 'im. Can't I see someone else?'

'I guess you can. You're a public patient, so your
notes will be held at the hospital. I'll ask Ren to
recommend someone better for you. OK?'

'Will he be there too? In Hobart?' Bertie's facial
expression altered from its usual scowl to one of hope.
Sarah had to gulp down the bubble of mirth which was
threatening to escape.

'You've taken a shine to him, haven't you?'

'What?' Bertie roared, the scowl firmly back in place.
'That outsider? Mind ya tongue, Sarah Rutherford.'

'As you wish,' Sarah replied meekly, still trying to
hide her smile.

'The question on everyone's lips is whether *you've*
taken a shine ta him. So, 'ave ya? You can tell me,
girlie. I'd not spread gossip round the town.'

This time Sarah did laugh out loud. 'You'll have to
wait and see. Now, as I'm here, I'll give you a quick
check-up. Have you been faithfully putting your
drops in?'

'Why do ya always ask me the same questions? I
dunno,' Bertie mumbled as she shuffled off toward her
bedroom, with Sarah close behind her.

'You know, Bertie, people in this town are too
inquisitive. After watching you for many years, I now
know exactly how to fend them off!'

'I'd be more than happy to recommend another ophthal-
mologist,' Ren said when Sarah explained the situation.

She'd found him in the kitchen and had come to the conclusion that he liked this room the most—especially when there was an empty plate with crumbs and a coffee-cup in front of him. 'When are you planning on booking her in?'

'As soon as possible or she'll change her mind. If I can persuade the hospital, I'd like to have her booked in for Monday morning. I'll have to cancel my clinic but it's fairly light at the moment and the patients won't mind being rescheduled.'

'I can always do your clinic.'

'Ren—' Sarah glared at him as though he were a small boy '—we've already discussed you and my clinics so let's not cover *that* ground again.'

'But no one turned up yesterday and I missed out on my fun,' he said grumpily, and Sarah laughed.

'Well, can you help me arrange Bertie's admission? You probably have a lot more influence with the staff at the hospital, so I'd appreciate your help.'

'Consider it done. Just remember that this is a favour to Bertie—not to you.' He grinned at her and she threw her arms in the air.

'What is it between you and her?' Sarah smiled teasingly at him. 'She was asking after you this morning. Wanted to know why you hadn't come with me. She seemed very disappointed.'

'Is that so?' He stood to take his plate and cup to the sink. 'Although I must admit that she took me off guard for a few moments I knew my natural charm would win her over. She's just the same as everyone else in this town.'

'In what way?' Sarah asked, feeling her hackles rise.

'Everyone here thinks I'm wonderful,' he stated with a nonchalant shrug.

Sarah buried her head in her hands and groaned. 'I think I'd better leave. There isn't enough room in this kitchen for me *and* your ego.'

Ren grinned. 'Things could have been worse.'

'What do you mean?' She lifted her head inquisitively.

'It could have been Mrs Birch that took the fancy to me. Then I'd be in big trouble.' He laughed and Sarah joined in.

'She's booked in to see me this afternoon so there should be some lovely scones or cake to have for our supper.'

He sighed and looked her straight in the eyes. 'You're very fortunate, Sarah. The townsfolk really appreciate you and do everything they can to help.'

'Well, the last thing they want is a disgruntled doctor who'll up and leave so I guess it's in their best interests to keep me happy.' She opened the refrigerator, looked disgustedly inside and closed it again. 'Did you eat *all* those pastries I brought back?'

Ren gave her an innocent look. 'Wasn't I supposed to?'

'No.' Sarah heard her front door open and close and realised that her first patient had arrived. 'Could you call Edith and ask her to bring lunch at twelve instead of one? I'm starving!' She shot him what she hoped was a chastising look but every time her eyes met his all she thought about was kissing him and her annoyance disappeared in a puff of smoke.

'I'd better get started on my clinic. Today is one day I don't want to run late.'

'Sure I can't help?'

'Not at the moment. Relax, read a book. If I need you I promise I'll call.'

He crossed the room and lifted her chin slightly. 'You do that,' he said and lowered his lips for a brief kiss. Sarah hadn't missed his double meaning and felt her body tingle with anticipation. 'Off you go and play doctor.' He turned her around and gave her a gentle push toward the door.

'If you insist,' she replied without enthusiasm, and went to call in her first patient.

Amazingly enough, the clinic ran almost on time, and after Sarah had eaten lunch she felt a lot better. Even Mrs Birch didn't stop for her usual long chat and, as predicted, she brought Sarah some freshly made scones.

'I'll pop them into the kitchen for you, shall I?' she asked while Sarah wrote up her notes.

'Thanks, Mrs Birch. That would be lovely.' Sarah smiled sweetly, knowing that she hadn't really come for a medical check-up at all but rather to check up on the dashing Dr Taylor. Unless Ren had decided to vacate the premises he'd be cornered with Mrs Birch for at least the next half-hour. Sarah's smile grew as she said good bye to her patient.

It was an hour later that Sarah heard a commotion in the lounge room that doubled as her waiting room. She was dressing Mr Entwhistle's burn from a frying-pan when loud shouts could be heard. She recognised one of the voices as belonging to Mr Cartwright, who was the eldest member of their town at ninety-seven. He was also one of the most argumentative males she had ever come across.

He had an opinion on everything and he was always right—regardless. He also thought that age gave him the prerogative to say what he thought, whether he hurt feelings, put noses out or generally annoyed the person concerned. Needless to say, though he was respected he wasn't very well liked.

'Excuse me, Mr Entwhistle,' Sarah said apologetically to her patient who was perched on her examination table, his hand resting on a sterile tray. 'I'll be back in a moment.'

'You go ahead, lassie. I know what old Cartwright's like when he sinks his teeth into something—or someone.'

Sarah left and met Ren in the hall. They entered the room together to discover that the 'someone' Mr Cartwright was taking a piece out of was fifteen-year-old Simon Jayton, one of Mike's younger brothers.

'What seems to be the problem?' Sarah asked calmly, although she had to raise her voice to be heard. They stopped their yelling and turned to face her—both speaking at once. She noticed that Simon was nursing his right arm and his forehead was beaded with sweat.

'This young whippersnapper thinks he can simply walk in here and jump the queue. That's not the way things are done, Dr Rutherford. I have an appointment and he doesn't. I'm too old to let people jump ahead of me. For all I know, if you saw him first I could quite probably be dead by the time my rightful turn came.'

Sarah nodded at Mr Cartwright, acknowledging his words, before walking over to the teenager. 'What have you done?'

'Fell off my skateboard.'

Sarah turned to Ren. 'Would you mind taking Simon through to the theatre? Looks as though this needs an X-ray.'

'Sure.' Ren quickly whisked Simon out of the room as Mr Cartwright opened his mouth to protest.

'You've just gone ahead and let him jump the queue.

It's unprofessional, Dr Rutherford, and quite frankly I expected more from a person of your standing in this community.'

'Mr Cartwright,' Sarah said, trying to keep her temper in check, 'Simon's arm is probably broken and he's in a lot of pain.' She held up her hand when the elderly man opened his mouth to protest.

'Dr Taylor is a qualified orthopaedic surgeon, visiting from Hobart, as I'm sure you've no doubt heard. He is the best person to deal with a broken arm. So, therefore, Simon hasn't really jumped any queue as Dr Taylor didn't have any patients scheduled for this afternoon.

'You were booked in to see me *after* Mr Entwhistle. I've almost finished my examination with Mr Entwhistle and will be out shortly to see you.' Sarah maintained her professional calm and waited for a few moments. Mr Cartwright simply nodded although it was obvious that he didn't want to concede defeat.

'Now, if you'll excuse me.' Sarah turned on her heel and left, rolling her eyes heavenward.

'All sorted out, lassie?' Mr Entwhistle chuckled when she returned and Sarah smiled, her frustration with the situation dissipating.

'Yes, thank you. Now let's finish dressing your hand before any more commotions arise.'

Mr Cartwright was as sweet as pie during his check-up and Sarah was glad to see him leave. She dug out Simon Jayton's file and took it through to the theatre. Simon was sitting on the barouche while Ren applied plaster of Paris to his arm.

Sarah looked at the X-rays that were hooked onto the viewer. 'Nice clean break of your forearm.'

'Yeah,' Simon grinned at her. 'What did you call it, Doc?'

'Your ulna. He fell clean onto it—unlike most people, who put their hand out to stop themselves from falling,' Ren said, looking over his shoulder at Sarah. 'Otherwise. . .' he turned his attention back to Simon '. . .you could have not only broken your ulna but your radius and wrist as well.'

'Wow. Three bones in one fall.' Simon seemed amazed.

'The radius is situated right next to your ulna.' Sarah held her own arm out palm upwards to show him where the two bones were.

'What's the upper part of the arm called?' Simon asked, his inquisitive nature getting the better of him.

'Your humerus,' Sarah replied.

'Please, Dr Rutherford,' Ren said with mock seriousness, 'now is not the time to be making jokes.'

Sarah laughed. 'Right. I'll leave you to it. If you wouldn't mind writing up Simon's notes, I'd appreciate it.'

'Sure. How many more to go?' Ren asked as she went to the door.

'Five and I'm almost to time. Miracle of miracles.' She raised her eyebrows for emphasis, knowing that Ren could sympathise with long clinics and the complications that usually arose.

Ren leaned back in his chair and rubbed his stomach. 'Edith should go into the catering business. That meal was wonderful—as usual.'

Sarah agreed and stood to clear the table. 'Do you ride?'

'You mean horse-ride?'

'Yes. How would you like to see more of the property from horse back?'

'Sounds great. There's just one small problem. What am I supposed to ride?' He stood, turned his chair around and straddled it. 'This chair?'

Sarah chuckled. 'If you like, although I'm sure Trevor wouldn't be averse to lending you one of his. A horse—not a chair,' she added quickly, and he grinned.

'I must warn you that I haven't ridden in at least ten years or more.'

'Good. That definitely gives me an advantage.'

Ren brought their glasses over to where Sarah was standing beside the sink. 'You prefer to have the upper hand, don't you?' he stated. 'Why?'

Sarah shrugged. 'I guess it gives me a feeling of control. Considering that I was raised with no affection from my father and then sent away to boarding school in Melbourne where I felt isolated, I tend to rely on my natural instincts. Being in control of a situation is one advantage that medicine has given me and I find that I would prefer the rest of my life to be structured that way.' She eyed him and nodded. 'You're exactly the same—domineering and making sure things are done your way. It's probably why we continually strike sparks off one another.'

'But we haven't had an argument for days.' He thought for a moment before clarifying, 'I mean a *real* argument.'

Sarah smiled. 'Not for the want of opportunities. I guess we've both been trying to control our tempers, besides, with the number of emergencies we've had to undergo, it's no wonder we've been on our best behaviour.'

'Is that what you think?' Ren took a step closer so that she was wedged between him and the bench. Placing an arm either side of her to ensure her complete captivation, Ren leaned even closer. 'I thought it was the chemistry between us that had stopped our heated, verbal sparring. Was I wrong?' His tongue flicked out provocatively to wet his lips, an action which Sarah's tongue mimicked.

She cleared her throat. 'I guess that might have something to do with it.' Her eyes kept darting from his mouth back to his eyes as the millimetres between them disappeared. She knew Ren could see the more rapid rise and fall of her chest as her pulse rate increased.

Finally, his lips met hers and Sarah groaned in willing submission. She'd missed the feel of them, the emotions his kisses evoked and, most of all, the feel of Ren's body pressed firmly against her own.

They clung to each other as the kiss intensified, growing in passion until Sarah thought that she would die from the love that was swelling within her heart. Ren pulled back, his breathing as erratic as hers, and looked down into her eyes.

'How about that ride before we get too carried away?' he suggested, and turned from her. Sarah felt cold without this body warmth but, after giving herself a little shake and discovering that her legs would support her, she moved towards him.

'Why do you keep calling a halt to things? Do you or don't you want a romantic involvement with me?' Sarah asked, completely bewildered by his start-stop actions to their intimacy.

'Sarah. . .' he reached out and put his hands on her shoulders '. . .things aren't always as black and white as they seem. There are. . .things about me that you don't know.'

'So, tell me,' she demanded, and was rewarded with a wry grin.

'If only it were that simple.' He let her go and ran a hand through his hair. 'I've never been able to trust people, especially after the way my parents rejected me. I want to trust you. . .'

'Then do it,' she urged, and he sighed.

'I'll try but these emotions don't come easily to me. You must be patient. Please?'

Sarah wanted to scream and shout—to break things, to kick things, to pummel his chest with her fists—but instead she took a deep breath and let it out very slowly. 'OK,' she nodded. 'Let's go for that ride and I'll tell you a bit about the property.'

Sarah rang Trevor to arrange a mount for Ren and said they'd be there in approximately twenty minutes. They enjoyed the walk over—but only after Ren had declined Sarah's offer of both of them riding across on Sebastian.

'Why did you name him that?' Ren asked as they ambled along, Sarah keeping a firm grip on Sebastian's reins.

She shrugged. 'I don't know—it just seemed to suit him.'

Ren smiled. 'My grandfather's name was Sebastian and he was the most regal and pompous man I'd ever met. He scared the living daylights out of me, much more so than my father ever did. If he'd known that a *horse* shared his name he'd probably have insisted that the animal be put to sleep.'

Sebastian whinnied at his words and Ren quickly apologised. Sarah grinned. 'He's very sensitive is my darling horse so mind your manners and watch what you say in future.'

'Noted,' Ren said seriously. 'Do you usually saddle him or ride bareback?'

'It depends on what kind of ride I'm going for. Usually when I ride in the evening I prefer to saddle him. Although he's used to night noises, if he did get spooked it would give me more control to calm him. But I must admit that I do enjoy riding him bareback and especially without reins. It's just the two of us and the countryside and we gallop into oblivion.'

'Sounds nice,' Ren said softly and reached for her free hand. He looked up at the sky. 'Looks as though we may get a storm tonight.' Grey clouds were gathering, although there were still some fluffy white ones around. They walked the rest of the way in silence, enjoying the evening breeze, as the sun slowly set and simply being in each other's company.

Trevor had Bluebell saddled and waiting for them when they arrived.

'Bluebell?' Ren raised his eyebrows and glared at Sarah. 'I'm supposed to ride a horse called Bluebell?'

'Yes, you are. You said you hadn't ridden in over ten years and Bluebell is a gentle mount who will obey your every command.' Sarah grinned at him. 'Besides, she's in love with Sebastian and will follow him to the ends of the earth.'

'I see,' he said as he placed his foot in the stirrup and levered himself up. 'Well, Bluebell, it looks as though you and I are meant to play follow-the-leader tonight.'

Sarah laughed and waved to Trevor. 'Ren thinks we're heading for a storm tonight so keep a close watch on Bluey.'

'Will do, missy. You two be careful, now.' Trevor waved back as they set off toward the far paddock.

'What's wrong with Bluey?' Ren asked as they ambled along.

'Although he lives with Edith and Trevor, every time there's a bad storm he somehow escapes from wherever they've put him and makes his way back to my house. It's as though the place provides security for him. Trouble is he's not getting any younger and the last time he came down in a storm he fractured his leg. I wish I could have him living with me permanently but it's unhygienic to run a practice with a dog coming in and out. Besides, I'm hardly ever at home.'

As they rode on Sarah explained what she could understand about the farming side of her property. 'I don't really have all that much to do with it and I'm fortunate to have people like Trevor and Edith whom I trust to run the place. If I could hand it all over to them tomorrow I would, but they don't want the land and we all seem happy with the status quo.'

'How many acres?'

'About a hundred and it's divided into crops, livestock and pasture land. From what I can tell, it's exactly the way my father set it up over forty years ago. Naturally improvements have been made but the subdivision of the land is still the same.'

The trotted on in silence for a while, Sarah slightly in front of Ren. She turned and looked over her shoulder. 'You're rather quiet. Is anything wrong?'

'Uh-uh,' Ren said slowly and shook his head. When his eyes met hers, they were filled with desire. 'I was just watching the way your body was swaying—it's hypnotising.' Bluebell let out a sigh and Ren chuckled. 'I'm with you, lady. Let's just hang behind and watch the scenery.'

Sarah blushed and gave a nervous laugh as she turned her attention forwards. 'Would you like to try a gallop, then?' She didn't give him any time to reply and, with a swift click of her tongue, she urged Sebastian on. As predicted, Bluebell followed at the same pace—whether Ren wanted her to or not.

It was almost two hours later that they returned to Sarah's home, mindful of the now-angry grey clouds that had blocked out the sky. After she'd tended to the horses she helped Ren into the house.

'I'm going to feel this tomorrow,' he groaned, and she gave him what she hoped was a seductive smile.

'I could always give you a massage. That should help.'

He grasped her hands in his. 'I'd love one but first I'll have a shower. You get the liniment ready and meet me in the lounge.' He hesitated before saying, 'It's safer there.'

Watching him go, Sarah felt her earlier bewilderment return. There was something that wasn't right. He obviously desired her, wanted her and seemed to need her, yet still she sensed him holding back. He hadn't given her any reasons for not being able to trust her and in a way she understood.

They had both been raised in a similar fashion but where Sarah had had the townsfolk to show her love and affection Ren had grown up with mild affection from nannies and that was all. No wonder his social interactive skills weren't so good.

If only she knew exactly how much time they would have together. From what she understood, his holiday was due to finish sometime next week and then where did that leave them?

He'd confessed a few days ago that he'd initially thought of engaging in a brief affair with her but something had happened to change his mind. Sarah knew that whatever that had been was the key to his unnatural resistance to the passion and chemistry which flowed freely between them.

Realising that her soul-searching had done her absolutely no good, she went to her consulting room in search of the liniment. She picked up the bottle and deposited it in the lounge, before going to her room to change.

She thought of wearing something feminine, knowing that it would drive Ren to breaking point. Looking through her cupboard, she discarded the idea as preposterous—especially when she had only a few old skirts and one dress to choose from.

She changed into a tracksuit and T-shirt and went to the lounge room. She found him lying in the middle of the floor, face down, on a blanket and stripped to the waist. He'd put on some relaxing music which gave the room a decidedly romantic air.

Her breath caught in her throat and her feet seemed glued to the floor. He was a magnificent specimen of a man, as she had thought on more than one occasion, and now her hands had the right to touch him. They tingled with anticipation as she slowly crossed the room and knelt down.

His elbows were pointing to the side and he rested his head on his hands. 'Be gentle with me, Sarah,' he whispered, not raising his head.

She rubbed her hands together to ensure that they were warm, before tipping some of the liquid onto her palm. His flesh was warm from his shower and Sarah found it hard to hold back the gasp that escaped her as she began to rub her hands over his back.

She closed her eyes and tried to focus on the technique of massage instead of the full-blooded man that lay at her mercy. His muscles were taut but slowly he began to relax under her ministrations.

Sarah knew her voice was husky as she said, 'Time to turn over.'

If she'd thought that massaging his back was torture it was nothing compared to his front. She poured more liniment onto her hands and slowly ran them up and down his rib cage. Clenching her teeth, she was determined to hold back any involuntary sound that escaped.

He still lay with his elbows to the side, the back of his head resting in his upturned palms, but this time his lids were half-open—watching every move Sarah made. She was beginning to get a headache from clenching her teeth so hard and she was positive that he could hear the loud thudding of her heart.

After a few more torture-filled moments Ren reached out and stilled her hands where they were caressing the flat of his stomach.

'Why did I ever think that this room would be safer than any of the others?' He shook his head before looking desirously at her. 'You're driving me wild, lady. How on earth do you expect me to relax?' His voice was as husky as hers had been and he gently pulled her down to him. 'I've tried to fight it—to give us more time—but I can't, Sarah.' He kissed her cheek, her neck and nibbled her earlobe. 'I want you—now!'

CHAPTER SEVEN

THIS was the decision that Sarah had been waiting for. Although it wasn't a declaration of Ren's undying love, it would suffice. He'd been holding back and now... now he was going to break free and take her with him.

Their lips met in heated, fiery passion—their tongues meshing together as they struggled to breathe with the intensity. His warm hands were on her back, pressing her into his chest, while her fingers raked through his hair.

Sarah closed her eyes in sweet rapture as his hand explored her body. Pulling the T-shirt from the elastic waist band of her tracksuit, Ren ran his hand over her flat stomach and up her ribs to cup one breast.

He groaned in frustration at the feel of her bra and, rolling her slightly toward him, he reached around and expertly flicked the catch undone. 'Isn't that better?' he whispered as his hand returned to its former position and lovingly caressed her flesh.

Sarah couldn't speak. She was being washed away on a tide of longing, of needing... She reached for his head and pulled him down to kiss her once more. His tongue ran a trail of fire around her lips before he claimed them for his own.

Lifting her T-shirt higher, Ren trailed small kisses down her neck then dipped his head to suckle sweetly on the rosy peak of her nipple. Sarah groaned in delight and arched her back, drawing his mouth deeper around her breast.

Feeling as though she might explode at any moment from desire, Sarah heard the storm outside break—the rain pelting down against the roof. She opened her eyes and saw a flash of light through the closed curtains and knew that that was exactly how she felt. As though she'd been hit by a bolt of lightning.

The wind picked up and began to howl around them as Ren turned his attention to her other breast. The sensations were incredible and Sarah didn't know how much longer she could stand this wondrous torture.

The sound of howling outside increased and Sarah's passion-filled mind slowly focused on the noise.

'Bluey!' She urged Ren off and jumped to her feet. Racing down the hall to the back door, Sarah opened it and assisted the old dog to haul its limp, wet body into the house.

'You crazy mutt,' she told the dog affectionately as she rubbed his head reassuringly. 'You're OK now.' His hind legs collapsed beneath him and he slumped down into a puddle on the floor.

'Is he all right?' a deep voice which was laced with humour said from behind her. She craned her neck to see Ren, leaning against the wall, one thumb hooked into his jeans pocket. It was a casual stance that she had seen him take many times over the past week but this time he looked even more handsome. Maybe it had something to do with his naked torso.

'Sarah? Is the dog hurt?' Ren reiterated his question.

'Ah. . .no.' She turned her attention back to Bluey and ran her hands over him. 'No, nothing seems to be broken. He's just shaken up and extremely wet. . . I'd better get him dry,' she said, as though convincing herself that this was the right thing to do—her first priority. What she really wanted to do was to adjourn to one of the bedrooms and pick up where they'd left off.

'There's plenty of time,' Ren said softly as he watched the emotions play across her face.

'Mind-reading, Dr Taylor?' Sarah asked and flushed scarlet as she straightened and noticed the disarray of her T-shirt and undone bra.

'It's not all that difficult.' Ren took a step forward and wrapped his arms around her. He once again reached for the catch of her bra and this time, hooked it together. 'Anything else I can assist you with?' He grinned down at her, before planting a kiss on her lips and releasing her.

'As a matter of fact, there is. You can help me bath Bluey. Also. . .perhaps you wouldn't mind. . .' She flicked her tongue over her lips and gave his figure a quick once-over, as though committing it to memory. 'Wouldn't mind putting a shirt on.'

Ren threw back his head and laughed. 'If you insist.'

'I do.' She looked down at the dog, then back to Ren. 'I'm. . .um. . .sorry we were interrupted. I didn't mean to just jump up in the middle of. . .um. . .and I don't want you to think that I didn't like. . .what you. . . were. . .' She trailed off as Ren began to laugh again. 'What?' she demanded. 'What's so funny?'

'You are.' He reached for her again and held her firmly as she began to struggle out of his grasp. 'I care about the dog's welfare as much as you do. There's no need to apologise, Sarah. As for knowing that you enjoyed my touch, well, let's just say it was obvious.' He kissed her again—more firmly, as though chastising her. 'Now, can we please organise poor Bluey before he contracts pneumonia?'

Sarah quickly called Edith to let her know that Bluey was safe and made her way to the laundry. They bathed the old dog who thanked them for their efforts by shaking himself from top to toe, drowning them in a deluge of water.

'That's the one thing about bathing dogs that I don't like,' Sarah laughed as she wiped herself down. 'Come on, fella, let's get you dry.' They rubbed him down with towels, making sure they stood back as he shook a lot of the water out all by himself.

'Do you have any dog food, here?'

'There's usually a tin in the cupboard next to the dishwasher.'

Bluey's ears picked up at the mention of food and he followed Ren into the kitchen, leaving Sarah to clear up the mess he'd made of her laundry.

By the time she'd finished it was almost ten-thirty and she was tired. Entering the kitchen, she yawned and Ren smiled at her.

'My sentiments exactly. I think we should call it a night—unless you want a cup of coffee or something to eat?'

'No way.' Sarah shook her head. 'Even if I were hungry I doubt if I could get my mouth to chew the food.' She looked down at Bluey who was licking his dish clean.

'Where does he sleep when he comes to visit?' Ren asked.

'On my bed.' Sarah's eyes met his and she sighed. 'So much for timing, eh?' He laughed and reached for her.

'A goodnight kiss and cuddle are definitely in order.' Ren bent his head to meet hers. The kiss was gentle and caring and Sarah found herself relaxing in his grasp. She rested her head on his chest, the thud of his regular heartbeat hypnotising her further.

'Off you go.' He kissed the top of her head. 'I'll lock up.' He turned her in his arms and urged her down the corridor to her bedroom. 'Don't let Bluey hog the bed,' he smiled as the dog settled himself in the centre. 'Sleep well,' he whispered and shut her door.

Sarah was up at the usual time and left to do her house calls. She hoped that they wouldn't take long as she was expecting her prototype to arrive in the morning's mail and was eager to hear Ren's comments.

Lizzie, however, wasn't as chipper as she'd been the past few mornings. Postnatal blues had hit with full force and when Sarah arrived she could hear raised voices—one male, one female and one baby.

No one heard her knock so she entered and walked in the direction of the noise. Reuben was in his pram in the kitchen while Lizzie and John stood at either end of the table hurling abusive words at each other.

Sarah picked the crying baby up and cuddled him close—her actions effectively stopping the two adults who were behaving abominably.

'Now that I have your attention,' she said quietly, 'please take a seat and we'll talk this through.'

'I've got to get to work,' John said, and took a couple of steps toward the door.

'Sit,' Sarah demanded, her voice still quiet but threaded with anger. 'You will stay and work this out with your wife even if it means losing your whole farm, John Dumar.'

Thankfully he did as he was asked and Sarah continued to walk back and forth with little Reuben whose tears were slowly subsiding. 'Lizzie,' Sarah asked as the other woman reached for yet another tissue and blew her nose, 'what's the problem?'

'I don't know,' Lizzie wailed.

'Oh, for crying out loud,' John said. 'She's been like this for the past five hours. I woke up to find her bawling her eyes out in bed.'

'There is nothing wrong with your wife, John. All pregnant women get postnatal blues a few days after having a baby. It's her hormones slowly returning to normal. . .' Sarah continued with her speech, while silently wishing she could knock both of their heads together.

It was over two hours later that she finished her calls and turned the car toward home. When she arrived there she found Ren, sitting in his favourite spot and eagerly examining the prototype.

'It's arrived,' she said, drawing up the chair next to him.

'I hope you don't mind me opening it,' Ren said sheepishly.

'Not at all. What do you think?'

'I've only just sat down with it. Say, how were the Dumars this morning? You certainly took your time.'

'Ugh. I'd rather not talk about it. Do you want another coffee?' She pushed her chair back and collected his empty cup from the table.

'That'd be great,' he replied, his attention focused on her device. 'This is really interesting, Sarah.'

'Thanks. Do you think the old Hound will go for it?'

'I'm not sure,' he said slowly, and Sarah frowned. 'It all depends on what's currently available or due to be released onto the market. Unfortunately, you can't patent ideas.'

Sarah had taken a sip of her coffee while he'd been talking and choked on it.

'What's wrong?' Ren looked up at her as she coughed.

She smiled at him. 'I was thinking the same thing the other night—that you can't patent ideas. I mean, I know you better than I did one week ago but what's to say you won't steal the idea for yourself?'

'Sarah!' Ren seemed offended by her words and Sarah quickly tried to clarify what she'd meant.

'I'm not saying that you would but what if you inadvertently mentioned the idea to a colleague and they took up on it? It would then be a race against time between me and someone else.'

He considered her words while she brought the coffee over and sat down. 'Does this,' he gestured to the prototype, 'mean that much to you?'

'It doesn't mean everything to me, but it means enough. It was something that worked for me in an emergency. When I returned to Australia I did some checking and found nothing similar on the market. So I decided—why not? Why not go for it and see what happens? I've never invented anything before so I guess it's been a real novelty for me as well as a learning experience.'

Ren nodded. 'What if. . .?' He stopped and took a sip of his coffee. 'Hypothetically speaking, of course. What if you discovered that there was something very similar to your device due to be released onto the market within the next two to three months?'

'But. . .' Sarah tried to interrupt but Ren held up his hand for silence.

'This other device had already gone through trials, FDA approval and has the engineering company all ready to proceed with mass production. How would you react?'

Sarah was quiet for a moment before answering honestly, 'I'd burst into tears. Is that what's happened? Is there a device like mine due to be released soon?'

'It was only a hypothetical question, Sarah. Let me have a closer look at this and make some discreet inquiries. In the meantime, you just relax.'

'OK. I guess I'd better get on with my paperwork before lunch. I've only got a small clinic this afternoon so would you like to go for another walk or ride?'

'Definitely a walk,' he laughed, and pretended to rub his backside. 'I don't think my muscles like me very much at the moment.'

Sarah gave him a quick kiss, before going to her consulting room and knuckling down to her administrative duties.

Sarah was just ushering her final patient out of the door when she heard the connection to her fax machine bleep. Returning to her desk, she made her notes in the file while she waited for the fax to stop rolling. Picking up the page, she did a double-take at the message printed there.

HAPPY BIRTHDAY, REN.

It was signed with numerous signatures and was on a Royal Hobart Hospital letterhead. Sarah smiled. It was good to know that Ren was well liked by his colleagues. Someone had written 'All the best for tomorrow' before signing their name. Not surprisingly, Sarah noted that the old Hound's signature didn't appear on the page. He probably couldn't be bothered to lower his standards to such a humane gesture.

So, it was Ren's birthday tomorrow. Sarah ran her finger and thumb along her chin and thought. There was no way that she could let the day go by without some sort of celebration. Picking up the phone, she quickly dialled Edith's number and told her.

'What do you think? Could we organise something at such short notice?' Sarah said in a conspiratorial whisper.

'I don't see why not. A lot of the townsfolk would be happy to chip in and bring some food along. I know everyone he's met thinks he's absolutely wonderful,' Edith gushed.

'Where should we hold it?'

'At the pub. I'll talk to Smithy tonight and organise things, as well as calling some of the ladies and asking them to help prepare a feast for our guest.' Edith giggled like a schoolgirl. 'Ooh, Sarah, this is so exciting. Trevor should be almost there with your meal so tell him to hurry home immediately.'

Sarah looked up as there was a knock on her consulting door. Ren didn't wait for her reply and stuck his head around. He nodded when he saw that she was on the phone, but instead of leaving he sauntered casually into the room. Sarah quickly dumped her file on top of the fax and said into the receiver, 'I'll be sure to tell him. Bye,' and hung up before Edith could say another word.

'Was that for me?' he asked, his eyebrows raised.

'No. It was Edith.' Sarah stood. 'She wants Trevor to go home straight away and not hang around here.'

'Right,' he nodded. 'That's what I came to tell you. He's just arrived.'

'Great.' Sarah made her way to the door, linking her arm with his. 'What's for dinner?' Before he could reply, she'd groaned and rolled her eyes in exaggeration. 'Please don't tell me it's pasta again!'

Ren smiled. 'I don't think so. Looks more like steak and kidney pie with vegetables.'

They passed on the message to Trevor who seemed

puzzled by the request. 'She didn't say what was wrong?' he asked Sarah.

'Not really. I'm sure it's not *that* urgent but what Edith wants Edith gets,' Sarah shrugged.

'Righto,' he said and bade them goodbye.

'There's a good movie on the TV tonight,' Sarah said while they ate. 'An old Cary Grant classic. Do you want to watch it with me?'

He studied her for a moment. 'Are you hoping for a repeat of last night's performance?'

'You mean, bathing a wet and muddy dog?' Sarah purposely misunderstood him.

'You know exactly what I mean,' he grinned at her. 'Or are you hoping that I'll keep my distance and we can simply enjoy each other's company?'

'That's the one,' she joked and then said more seriously, 'I think you're right, Ren. It's important for us to get to know each other more thoroughly before we move onto the physical side of the. . .relationship.' There was no way that Sarah wanted him to seduce her tonight. Edith would probably call her a few times to discuss things and she refused to be interrupted *again* when she and Ren were finally joined together in a passionate union.

The movie on TV was her only hope of keeping him occupied while her mind worked overtime on the rushed preparations for tomorrow—coming up with ideas to make it special for him.

'Cary Grant?' He seemed to be thinking it over very seriously. 'Sounds harmless enough.'

'Great!' Sarah took a sip of her drink. 'Now tell me exactly what you think of my prototype.'

A strange look crossed his face and Sarah thought that it was embarrassment. Why would Ren be embarrassed about giving an opinion on her device. . .unless. . .

'What's wrong? Don't you think it has potential?'

He pretended to be interested in his meal, before finally looking up to meet her eyes. 'It has great potential, Sarah.' His voice was soft and radiated encouragement.

'Why do I get the feeling that there's a big "but" coming up?'

'Because there is. It may need a few modifications for the purpose you intend. Before I can make a further judgement I'd need to take it to one of our biomedical labs and run some tests on it.'

'Do you think the old Hound would be interested in seeing it?' Sarah asked hesitantly.

Ren looked thoughtfully at her for a moment, before slowly nodding his head. 'Maybe it would be better if I showed him when I return to work.'

Sarah felt uneasy at his words. Had she misjudged him?

'Trust me, Sarah,' he said, obviously reading the expression that crossed her face. 'I would never steal another colleague's work. If *I* present your case to the. . .old Hound, and recommend tests, then he should have no trouble granting his permission for the tests to go ahead. The people who work in our labs are employed to do a specific job, and any other work should be done out of hours and with you having to foot the bill for the time and expertise.'

They were both silent for a few moments while Sarah mentally weight the pros and cons of what Ren was suggesting. It was almost as though she was admitting defeat when she finally agreed.

'OK. You can take it and perform the tests. I'd prefer it if the design specifications stayed here but you can take the prototype.' Her shoulders sagged and Ren reached over and took her hand in his.

'Trust me, Sarah,' he reiterated.

They settled down to watch the movie and afterwards went to their separate bedrooms. Sarah's mind was caught up in her prototype and consequently she found it hard to sleep. Was Ren right? Was she wrong in taking the chance to trust him with something as valuable as this? She agreed that more tests needed to be done and if Ren could swing it so that the biomedical labs did them during working hours she would be grateful.

If only she'd had a chance to see the old Hound, she thought, thumping her pillow in frustration. To get his expert opinion would be beneficial in helping her to decide what to do next. Even though she didn't like what she'd heard about him, or the way his secretary kept finding excuses for him not to meet with her, Sarah knew that, whether his advice was in her favour or not she'd take it.

Think about something else, she told herself sternly. Ren's party. Edith had called her only once that evening and just in case Ren could overhear her conversation, even though she'd been in the kitchen and he in the lounge room, Sarah had answered in monosyllables. Thankfully, Edith had guessed what she was trying to do and had asked her questions which only needed a yes or no answer.

'Who was that?' he'd asked when she'd returned to the lounge and settled down next to him. 'Was it an emergency?'

Sarah had laughed nervously, trying to make light of the situation. 'No, no. Not an emergency. Just a friend. I told you that the townsfolk usually give me the week-end off and save their ailments for Mondays.'

They'd resumed watching the movie and after another ten minutes—when Sarah had realised that he wasn't going to question her further—she'd begun to relax, enjoying the comforting feel of Ren's arm about her shoulders.

She sighed in remembrance, pummelled her pillow again and turned over, untangling the bedclothes from her legs and setting them to rights. Considering that the weather forecast for the following day was for beautiful sunshine and a warm night with no rain, Edith had suggested having a barbeque at the pub.

Smithy had agreed to the use of his premises and several of the ladies were prepared to assist with the catering arrangements.

'Why don't you take him on a picnic tomorrow after-noon and show him a bit of the countryside?' Edith had suggested. 'We'll need to have him out of the way just in case he begins to ask questions. That will ensure that we *really* surprise him.'

'OK.' Sarah had agreed and so she was scheduled to go on a picnic with Ren. More time alone...just the two of them. She hoped that she'd be able to keep her desire under control—and her emotions. The other night, when he'd been stirring up the storm within her while the weather had whipped one up outside, Sarah had felt the declaration of her love for him springing to her lips. She wondered what his reaction would have been if she'd said it.

He seemed confused and sometimes even distant when he was fighting the emotions he felt for her. There was something wrong, and Sarah had no idea what it was. He'd told her to trust him with regard to her device, but what about her heart?

The final days spent with her father, combined with

the love and support of the community over the years, had helped Sarah over the worst of her fear to trust people but, as far as she was concerned, she still had a long way to go.

Stop letting your thoughts run wild, she told herself sternly. Relax and get some sleep. Easier said than done, she thought an hour later when she was still tossing and turning. Eventually Sarah drifted off into a troubled sleep only to be woken by her alarm clock, urging her to begin the day.

Grumbling to herself, she threw back the bed covers and made her way into the kitchen for some coffee. She found Ren, sitting at the table, and freshly brewed coffee waiting for her.

'You look exactly the way I feel,' he commented wryly as he watched her cross the room to pour herself a cup. 'Maybe we're not doing ourselves any favours by ignoring the attraction between us.'

Sarah almost snorted her coffee as the irony of his words hit her. Last night had been the first night since he'd arrived that she hadn't dwelled on the attraction between them. Instead she'd lain awake, thinking about trusting him with her device. What kind of a woman was she?

'Something wrong?' he queried, but Sarah shook her head and joined him at the table.

'I've had an idea,' she said, and gave him a playful punch on the arm when he gasped in mock amazement. 'Why don't we drive up to Launceston today? It's just over an hour and I know a great café where we can eat. Not as good as Café Lella but almost. Are you tempted?'

'What about being on call?'

'Today people will simply have to do without the doctor and her sidekick.' Ren pulled a face at the name she'd given him but Sarah ignored it. 'So, how about it?'

'Sure,' he nodded. 'When do you want to leave?'

'As soon as possible. If my stomach can hold out for another hour we can have breakfast there.'

'Fine. Do you want the shower first?' His voice held a note of promise, as though he would even be willing to share it with her.

'No,' Sarah said after a moment's hesitation. 'You go ahead. I'll call Edith and let her know not to prepare any food for us today.' It would also give her the opportunity to get an update, without worrying about Ren overhearing.

They spent a wonderful day in Launceston and as Ren had only been to Launceston twice—both times for conferences—Sarah took delight in showing him around.

The temptation to take in a movie was too great to refuse and they laughed their way through the latest Steve Martin release.

'It's been a wonderful day,' Ren said to Sarah as they began the drive home. 'I can't remember when I've enjoyed myself so much. Thank you.' He took her hand off the steering-wheel and kissed it.

'I feel exactly the same way—so thank *you*.' She grinned at him, before inserting a cassette into her tape-player. The relaxing sounds of Strauss filled the air and Ren looked at her in surprise.

'I thought you liked Billy Joel?'

'I do. It doesn't mean that I don't like other types of music as well.'

'You're a constant source of surprise,' he said, and leaned his head back against the head-rest and dozed. Sarah took more than one chance to snatch a glimpse of him as he sat there, breathing deeply, the lines on his face relaxed and content. He looked so different tonight from the way he had this time last week.

He woke as she turned the vehicle off the main road, and apologised for sleeping.

'Think nothing of it. Besides, I enjoyed hearing you snore.'

'I do not snore,' he stated emphatically as he stretched his arms up and flexed them against the roof.

'How much do you want to bet?' she joked. As they drove into the main street of the town it was lit up like a Christmas tree.

'What's going on here?' Ren sat forward in his seat and looked out of the windscreen. 'Is this some town festival or something?'

'Or something,' Sarah answered, pulling the car to a halt. She released her seat belt and jumped out before he could ask any more questions. She came around to his side of the car and took his hand in hers.

'Come on, let's go and investigate.' Although the street was lit up there was no sign of life. Sarah led an inquisitive Ren over to the pub and as they walked in the door people jumped out from every nook and cranny shouting, 'Surprise!' They then broke into a chorus of 'Happy Birthday'.

Ren didn't know where to look and his grip on Sarah's hand tightened. He thanked everyone for their best wishes, before leaning down to whisper in Sarah's ear, 'This was all your doing wasn't it?'

She looked up into his face and smiled. 'You bet.'

'What if I told you that I hate surprise parties?'

'I'd say, tough—it's too late.'

He gave her a smile and hugged her close to him. 'Thanks, Sarah. No one has ever done anything like this for me before. How can I ever repay you?'

'I'm sure we can come to some arrangement,' she said and in front of the whole room Sarah stood slightly on tiptoe and kissed him—one great, big smacking kiss.

CHAPTER EIGHT

THE festivities continued to roll on and Ren graciously accepted the best wishes for his birthday. Sarah produced the fax which had been sent from his colleagues in Hobart and realisation dawned in his eyes.

'So this is how you knew,' he stated. 'I was wondering whether you'd gone through my belongings and found some hidden clue.'

'Ren,' Sarah said in mock horror. 'How could you suspect me of such a thing?'

'I wouldn't have put it past you when I first arrived.' He said his arm around her. 'This is a great party.'

'Edith organised most of it. My job was to keep you occupied.'

'Well, you're certainly good at your job.'

There was a loud crash at the opposite end of the room and immediately conversations stopped as everyone looked round.

Ren's and Sarah's feet both took flight as they saw Hilda Birch, lying on the floor with the trestle table collapsed beneath her.

'Hilda!' Sarah called and received no response. She reached for the limp, frail wrist and found no pulse. Ren checked her pupils—again there was no response.

'I suspect a myocardial infarction,' Sarah mumbled, and received a brief nod from Ren. He tipped Hilda over onto her side to check that she hadn't swallowed her tongue.

'Myo- what?' Bertie blustered. 'For cryin' out loud, girl, speak English.'

'A heart attack, Bertie,' Sarah informed her. 'Could everyone please move back to give us some room. Trevor,' she called over her shoulder, unsure of exactly where he was, 'I'll need oxygen, a stretcher, my bag and get that plane ready.'

While Sarah was talking, Ren had tilted Hilda's head back, pinched her nose, secured her chin and had breathed five breaths into her mouth. Sarah knelt alongside Hilda's body, linked her hands together, placed them over the old lady's breastbone and began cardiac compression.

There was no noise in the room except for Sarah's voice as she counted out the rhythm of cardiopulmonary resuscitation. After her fifth compression Ren breathed into Hilda's mouth—the elderly woman's chest rising and falling as he did so.

They seemed to have been working for ages when in reality it was just under a minute. The silence around them became deafening but Sarah and Ren concentrated on the task at hand. After the minute was up Ren indicated that they should change positions. They swapped with all the expertise their training had afforded them and Ren counted out the rhythm.

Almost at the end of the second minute Hilda had a faint carotid pulse and gave a very weak cough. Between them, Sarah and Ren gently manoeuvred Hilda into the coma position, before standing to stretch out their bodies.

Everyone expelled a sigh of relief, then broke out into a spontaneous round of applause. 'Well done,' people called, some patting Ren on the back. They waited for Trevor, who had taken Mike with him, to arrive with the oxygen which was promptly fitted over Hilda's mouth.

'Don't struggle.' Sarah's voice was soft as she stroked the woman's hair. 'You'll be just fine, Hilda. Take deep breaths and relax.' Hilda's eye lids fluttered at Sarah's words, indicating that she'd heard.

Her pulse was stronger than before but Sarah still kept a close eye on the situation as Hilda was laid on the stretcher and carried out of the room.

'The tablets didn't work,' Hilda managed to whisper through the oxygen mask once they had her settled at Sarah's house.

'Shh. It's all right. I'm organising to take you to Hobart so you can be checked by a specialist. Edith will pack any necessary things you need and bring them over before we leave.' Sarah looked up as Ren opened the door and wheeled in the ECG machine.

'We're going to hook you up to this machine which monitors your heart's movements. It doesn't hurt at all and it will give us an indication of any damage caused by your collapse. I'll also give you an injection for the pain, which should help you to relax.'

Hilda's eyes widened as Sarah spoke but she nodded, indicating her consent. Tears began to shimmer in her eyes and Sarah stroked her forehead. 'It's all right, Hilda. You're doing fine.'

'The children. . .' she whispered.

'I'll contact them. They'll be able to visit you in hospital and spoil you rotten. Now, isn't that something to look forward to?' Sarah said with a bright, reassuring smile on her face. They waited for the first print-out, before tearing it off and leaving Hilda to rest.

She crossed the hallway to her consulting room, read the thin report and handed it to Ren who was directly behind her. 'She's damaged some tissue,' Sarah said, shaking her head, and dropped into a chair. Ren raised his eyebrows, before following her example and sitting down.

'You know, contrary to what you might believe, I don't usually have this much excitement in so short a time. Everything comes in droves or it doesn't come at all. Why can't emergencies happen all nicely spaced out?'

'It would make a life a little easier,' he agreed. 'I guess that's one advantage of working in a hospital. At least you can go home at the end of your shift and leave someone else to take over the problems.'

'You'd still be on call, though,' Sarah felt compelled to point out.

'Sure, but *you're* on call twenty-four hours a day—seven days a week. At least I get the odd weekend free.' He paused and raised a hand to his chin. 'Although, I must admit that after the time I've spent here, I thoroughly enjoy the country. Admittedly, I enjoy hiking and walking and that kind of thing for recreational purposes but that was the only reason I ever went bush. Now that I've had a chance to see a country GP at work, I can appreciate the work you do and the relationships you have with your patients.'

'You almost sound surprised at your conclusions,' Sarah smiled at him and was awarded with a heart-stopping grin.

'I am. When I arrived here I couldn't think of anything worse than being trapped in such a small town for more than twenty-four hours.'

'What made you change your mind?' Sarah asked, and held her breath, waiting for his answer.

His smile faltered for a moment before he answered,

'A number of reasons. Do you think Hilda's going to be well enough to fly?'

Changing the subject, eh? Well, she'd let him—just this once. 'She should be. I'll keep an eye on her for the next hour and if there's no change we'll take her in. I would feel happier if you'd come with me. If she arrests while we're flying there'd be a better chance of pulling her through if there are two of us.'

He was silent, as though weighing up the pros and cons of her suggestion. 'I'd rather not but. . .considering the circumstances. . .I have little choice.'

'Can you tell me why you'd rather not go? I can always get Edith or Mike to come with me.'

'No, it's fine. It would be better if the two of us were there. I just don't want to return to Hobart until I absolutely have to.'

'It might burst your bubble?'

'Something like that.'

'If you'd rather not come to the hospital you can stay with Trevor and the plane while the ambulance transfers us, and once the admit is over and done with I'll come straight back then we can return immediately. How's that sound?'

'Better. Thank you.'

'My pleasure,' she replied, running her tongue over her lips in a provocative gesture.

'Go and check your patient,' he ordered, and shook his finger at her. 'You're playing doctor at the moment—not seducer.'

Sarah stood and snapped her fingers. 'Darn it, I forgot.' She walked over to where he sat and stood in front of him—her breasts level with his eyes. She jutted her chest out further and whispered as sensuously as she could, 'When *can* I play seducer?'

Ren tilted his head to look up at her, his face brushing the tip of one breast as he did so. 'Soon,' he answered, desire burning in his eyes. 'Very soon.'

The transfer went without a hitch and it was in the early hours of Sunday morning that Ren and Sarah crawled into bed. Too exhausted to even consider seduction, they both slept until late.

After Sarah's visit to the Dumar household she slumped down at the kitchen table and eagerly drank the coffee Ren placed in front of her.

'Everything OK?'

'Fine.' Sarah ran a hand through her hair. 'Not only do I need a district nurse, I also need a social worker.'

Ren chuckled. 'I'm glad you're at least realising that you need help.'

'I've thought a lot about it since you arrived. Just having an extra person around with medical training has made all the difference.'

'Extra person,' he mumbled. 'Is that all I am to you? An extra person?'

Sarah looked him directly in the eyes. Although he was teasing she couldn't resist asking, 'What would you prefer to be?'

'That's a loaded question,' he answered softly. The phone rang and he snatched it up. 'Doctor's residence,' he snapped, a frown creasing his forehead. 'Just a minute.' He punched the 'hold' button and held the receiver out to Sarah. 'I'm really beginning to hate your phone. Every time I try to talk to you. . .'

'Or seduce me,' she interrupted with a grin.

'Or seduce you,' he added, 'that stupid phone can't resist ringing its head off.'

She took the receiver from him. 'How can you hate

an inanimate object, Ren?' she teased.

He shook his head in disgust. 'I'm going to take a shower—a cold one,' he added, before stalking out of the room. Sarah chuckled to herself, before retrieving the caller.

'Dr Rutherford speaking.' It turned out to be an old schoolfriend, ringing from Melbourne, and by the time Ren had finished his shower, dressed and had another two cups of coffee Sarah decided that it was time to conclude her call.

'About time you got off that contraption,' he growled, and Sarah laughed.

'What's your problem?

'I don't know. I feel. . .restless. I knew I shouldn't have gone to Hobart last night.'

'But you stayed with the plane so, in reality, you only went to Hobart airport,' Sarah felt compelled to point out. They heard a 'yoo-hoo' from the direction of the back door. 'Here's Edith,' Sarah said unnecessarily. 'Better put your happy face on. . .' she teased as she welcomed her neighbour, who had arrived with a mountain of sandwiches for their lunch.

'So,' Sarah asked when she'd stuffed herself, 'what would you like to do with the rest of the day?'

'My guess is that we should stay here and wait for that phone to ring. The way I figure it you should be due for another emergency in approximately. . .' he checked his watch '. . .another five hours. I wonder what it will be this time.' He rubbed his hands together in anticipation. 'I can hardly wait.'

Sarah eyed him and shook her head. He wasn't joking this time—he was serious. 'If you'd rather return to Hobart I'm sure that could be arranged.' She strove to keep her voice from breaking and only just succeeded.

They stared at each other for a few seconds before Ren banged his fist on the table in frustration.

'I'm sorry, Sarah. I can't expect you to understand the predicament I find myself in.'

'Try me,' she said softly.

He looked at her and opened his mouth, as though to speak, then shut it again.

'You're a fish?' she guessed—trying to lighten the mood. It didn't work.

The phone rang and Sarah jumped up to get it. 'I thought the phone wasn't suppose to ring for another couple of hours.'

'Maybe it's another friend,' she heard him grumble as she lifted the receiver.

'Dr. . .' Sarah didn't even have time to finish speaking before the voice on the other end drowned her out.

'Doc.' The urgent voice belonged to Patrick Jayton, Mike's father. 'It's Mike. He's had a terrible accident. The tractor's over turned and he's trapped underneath. I think. . .I think he's dead.'

'I'm on my way.' Sarah replaced the receiver and stalked out of the kitchen into her consulting room. Ren followed and found her throwing anything and everything into her black doctor's bag. She glanced up at him. 'I wish you'd been right. I wish it was another friend, ringing for a chat. Mike Jayton's trapped under a tractor. His father thinks he's dead.' She placed a call to Ed and Kate, before rushing out of the house.

It took less than five minutes for Sarah and Ren to reach the accident site. Patrick ran over to them, his voice filled with hope.

'He's groaning, Doc. He's not dead—my boy's alive!'

'Mike,' Sarah called as she dropped to her knees, not

caring how muddy the ground was. 'Mike, it's Sarah. Can you hear me?' She held her breath and waited for a reply. It finally came—muffled and faint.

'Good. We're going to get you out, Mike, but I need you to tell me where it hurts the most.' She needed to keep him talking while they moved the tractor off him—he must be conscious. Patrick had phoned a number of neighbours, Trevor being one of them, and the men—who were just arriving—would soon be able to free young Mike. 'Mike,' Sarah called again when she received no reply. He seemed to be slipping in and out of consciousness. 'Mike, where does it hurt?'

'My arm—I can't move my arm.'

'Which one?' Sarah raised her voice so that he could hear her.

He paused, as if trying to distinguish left from right. 'The right one. . . And my legs—I can't move them.'

'Don't try. Just lie completely still and keep talking to me.' The men were hooking ropes and chains around the tractor, getting ready to lift it. Ren knelt down beside her.

'What's the story?'

'Could be anything. He says he can't move his legs. . .'

'Spinal damage?'

'Possibly. Right arm is also sore—let's hope it's just a fracture.'

'If it is spinal we'll be in Theatre for the rest of the day,' he stated as he straightened up. 'And to think I was complaining of restlessness.' He ran a hand through his hair, before going to help with the tractor.

Sarah kept talking to Mike while the tractor was slowly levered from him. The moment it was clear, both Sarah and Ren shifted to the boy's side. Sarah swabbed his left arm and injected a shot of pethidine for pain relief.

Ren examined Mike's legs and pelvis and breathed a sigh of relief. 'Doesn't appear to be any spinal damage, although the pelvis is fractured. I'll need it X-rayed, as well as his arm.'

'Pulse, BP, and pupil activity all correspond to trauma. Are you ready to have him moved?'

'Let me just finish checking his arm,' Ren said as he moved towards Mike's right shoulder. 'Dislocated,' he announced and looked down into Mike's face. 'We'll get you into theatre and fix you up.'

The stretcher was brought over and Mike was strapped securely to it, before loading him into the four-wheel-drive.

'Doc.' Patrick came over to her as she was preparing to leave. 'What's wrong with him? Will he be all right?'

'He's dislocated his shoulder,' Ren informed him before Sarah could open her mouth.

'Can't you just put it back in?'

'No. It could be fractured, in which case we'd need to operate on it. He's also broken his wrist—what we call a Colles' fracture. His pelvis is also broken, and exactly what we'll find there we won't know until he's been thoroughly X-rayed.' He turned to Sarah. 'Don't suppose you have 3D scanning facilities?'

'Sorry—that's about the one thing I don't have.' She knew he was only joking and trying to lighten the mood as the facilities for three-dimensional scanning were extensive. Sarah would probably have to build another room simply to house it.

'You'll need to come with us, Patrick, to sign the consent form. Mike's only seventeen and, as his legal guardian, we can't operate without your signature. Will the other children be OK by themselves for a while?'

'Yeah. Simon will look after them. I'll just let him know what's happening and catch up to you.'

'What happened to his wife?' Ren asked quietly as he sat with Mike and monitored him while Sarah drove.

'She walked out on him when the youngest was eight. She's been gone for almost three years and the family are coping quite well without her.'

'How many children?'

'Five. Mike's the eldest, then Simon who's fifteen. The twin girls are next, Gracie and Alison—they're thirteen—and then there's Tommy who's now eleven. Patrick has coped remarkably well—considering.' Sarah gently eased the car to a stop.

'I'll begin preparations and get scrubbed,' Ren told her, and she nodded. She was met by Trevor and a few other men who assisted in unloading Mike. Both Ed and Kate were busy at their jobs when they transferred him to the barouche. She rechecked his vital signs, noting her findings on the chart. Patrick walked through the open door, calling to her as he did so.

'In here,' she replied, and he poked his head into the preparation area.

'Mike. . .son,' he said brokenly, and walked over to the barouche. 'You'll be fine, lad. The doc's going to take good care of you.'

'But the farm. . .' Mike said through his drug-induced haze.

'Don't worry about that, son. Simon and Tommy will be able to help and I'm sure some of the blokes in town will lend a hand until you're up on your feet again.' He clasped his son's uninjured hand firmly, before letting it go. It was an emotional scene yet neither one of them had a glimmer of a tear in their eyes.

'Patrick. . .' Sarah held the consent form out to him '. . .if you wouldn't mind signing this, we'll be able to start.'

Patrick signed the form and left after Sarah had promised to contact him the minute they were finished in Theatre.

They X-rayed Mike's shoulder and wrist, before doing the more complex X-rays required for his pelvic fracture. Ren studied the X-rays in great detail. 'The pelvis looks as though it won't need surgical intervention. There's no fracture with his dislocated shoulder so it's simply a matter of relocating it back into place. The Colles' fracture needs to be reduced before enclosing it in a plaster cast. Once we've done that we can rig up traction for his pelvis and organise for him to be transferred to Hobart.'

Sarah nodded in agreement. 'Bertie's going to Hobart as an elective admission tomorrow so we may as well transfer them both at once. No point in doing an extra trip when we don't have to.'

'Agreed. Ed. . .' Ren turned to the elderly gentleman '. . .we're ready to anaesthetise.'

The shoulder was relocated into position before they started on his wrist. Reducing the fracture involved Ren pulling the bone so that it was in the correct position, before applying local moulding pressure to realign the bone.

Sarah mixed up the plaster of Paris and watched Ren apply it with the bandage. It was a routine task but he performed it with such speed and precision that Sarah was impressed.

They transferred Mike from the operating table back to the barouche, which was easily fitted with traction bars. They pushed Sarah's bed aside and wheeled him into her room. That way she could monitor him more easily through the night. She called Patrick and told him the news, before writing up Mike's notes.

'Edith's brought dinner over for all of us. It's piping hot and ready to eat.' Ren was leaning against the doorframe. 'So, how about coming and putting some food into your stomach before you start cleaning that theatre?' It was an order—not a question. He walked over to her desk, removed the pen from her hand and, after pulling her up from her chair, led her by the shoulders into the kitchen.

'Sit—eat.'

'You certainly are bossy,' she retorted and breathed in the wonderful smell of beef Stroganoff.

'How do you think I got to be profess—' He stopped in mid-sentence and quickly coughed. 'Professionally successfull,' he finished. 'Aren't all professionals bossy?'

'It depends,' Sarah answered suspiciously. She frowned and concentrated on her food, not wanting to meet his eyes. What had he just tried to cover up? She decided that enough was enough and looked up from her meal—ready for a confrontation.

'Ren, there's something you're not telling me. You've been encouraging me to trust you with regard to my device, and I'm willing to take that risk. I'm also willing to take the risk of trusting you with my heart.'

He looked at her and she knew that she had his full attention. 'I'll admit that I didn't like you much at first, but the more time I've spent with you. . .the more I found myself falling. . .in love with you.'

'Sarah. . .'

'No, please. . .' she held up her hand to silence him '. . .I can't change the way I feel, Ren. Trust involves

a risk and I'm willing to take that, but are you? We
haven't known each other for very long but with the
amount of time we've been spending in each other's
pockets, both professionally and socially, I find myself
with no other option than to offer you my love. Please
talk to me—confide in me.' She whispered the last few
words, never breaking eye contact.

The clock ticked on as she waited patiently for him
to speak. She watched his eyes reflect different emotions—from desire and wanting to complete
withdrawal. The shutters were firmly in place when he
spoke, his voice rough.

'I can't, Sarah. What you're asking is impossible. I
didn't ask for you to fall in love with me, nor have I
done anything to encourage such an emotion. Lust
maybe, but not love.' He pushed his chair back and
stood. 'I'm sorry.' He didn't sound sorry, Sarah thought
as she watched him walk around the table and leave
the room.

Seconds later she heard the door to his room being
firmly shut, just as he was firmly shutting her out of
his life—his heart.

Sarah avoided Ren as much as possible the next morning. Through the night she'd concentrated all her
energies on Mike and his condition. She left early and
went to see the Dumars, before continuing on to
Bertie's place.

'Are ya sure I have ta have this stupid operation?'
Bertie grumbled as Sarah carried her small overnight
bag to the car. 'And why do I have ta pack a bag? You
told me it was day surgery and that I'd be home by
tonight.'

'It's simply a precaution,' Sarah pacified her, and

helped the old woman to climb into the four-wheel-drive.

'Against what?'

Sarah turned in the driver's seat to look at her passenger. 'Are you going to grumble the entire time?'

'Yep. So get used ta it, girlie. Now, tell me what's 'appened with young Mike Jayton. Is he OK?'

'He's stabilised. Thankfully he will also be on the plane going to Hobart so I can ignore you and talk to him if I want to,' Sarah retorted, aware of her impertinence but not caring in the slightest.

'Got ya knickers in a knot over somethin', haven't ya?' Bertie asked, her eyes narrowing perceptively.

'No.'

'Suit yaself.' Bertie turned and watched the scenery go by as Sarah drove back to her house. Trevor was waiting for them in the kitchen but there was no sign of Ren.

'Haven't seen him today, missy,' Trevor informed her. 'Ready to load your patients onto Rudolf?'

'Ready as I'll ever be,' Sarah said, trying to inject a bit of enthusiasm into her voice. Where was he? She would have thought he'd be around to supervise Mike's transfer to the plane. Sarah's heart plummeted directly into her shoes and stayed there for the entire journey to Hobart.

'So which doc am I seein'?' Bertie asked as they travelled by ambulance from the airport to the hospital.

'Dr Anderson. Ren arranged everything for you and said he's the best ophthamologist he knows.'

'Well, that's all that matters, eh? If your Dr Taylor says he's good, then I'll go quietly.'

Sarah laughed for the first time that day. 'You make it sound as though you're headed for the electric chair.'

'That's how it feels,' Bertie replied gloomily.

When they arrived at the hospital Mike was transferred to the orthopaedic ward and Bertie was wheeled
off in a wheelchair to Ophthalmology day surgery. She
didn't take too kindly to being separated from Sarah
and kicked up a stink.

'Bertie, I have to go and admit Mike, then I'll be
right back by your side. Be nice to the staff or I'll make
sure they don't use an anaesthetic at all.' Sarah knew
that the threat would work, though they both knew that
she'd never carry it out, and Bertie seemed content to
grumble quietly to herself. Sarah was certain she heard
her say, 'If it weren't for ya father,' as they wheeled her
away. She smiled and made her way to Orthopaedics.

Once the hand-over was complete, Sarah took the
opportunity to go and visit her other patients. She felt
as though she was doing a ward round as she saw Ruby
Maddox and Margaret Braithwaite in the women's surgical department before going down to ICU to check
on Hilda Birch.

She was just leaving the small isolation cubicle when
a white-coated doctor stopped her in the corridor.

'You're not supposed to be here,' the brisk voice said
and she turned to confront him.

'Kevin!' she said in surprise. He'd been the anaesthetist the night Ren had arrived. She saw that his face
reciprocated her emotion.

'Sarah! What are you doing here?'

'Admitting a few patients and checking up on others,'
she replied.

He nodded and smiled. 'So, how are you coping with
the old Hound?'

Sarah gave him a puzzled look. How did he know

she had been trying to see Professor Fox-Taylor? 'I don't understand,' she replied.

'Ren. I thought he was still staying with you—at least, that's what his secretary told me. We sent a fax to him for his birthday—just to rub in the fact that he was turning forty, although he'd skin us all alive if we actually mentioned his age.'

Sarah felt her head begin to spin and put a hand up to her forehead. 'You mean to tell me that Ren and Professor Fox-Taylor are one and the same person?'

'Yeah. Ridiculous name,' Kevin continued, seemingly unaware of Sarah's distress. 'Lawrence Montgomery Sebastian Fox-Taylor. Amazing that someone could actually be called that—but it's true. We used to joke with him in med school that his monogram looked like an eye chart.'

Sarah reached out a hand to the wall to steady herself but was too late. The ground rushed up to meet her as she collapsed on the floor.

CHAPTER NINE

'SARAH!' She heard her name being called and opened her eyes, to find herself looking at a white ceiling. 'Sarah!' She turned her head in the direction of the voice and slowly focused. Kevin's face loomed into view.

'Are you all right?'

'Fine.' She tried to sit but felt her head begin to swim. Lying back on the pillow, she asked softly, 'Where am I?'

'I brought you into the treatment room. Just lie still.' He had one hand on her wrist and was counting the beats of her pulse. 'That's better. Have you any idea what caused you to faint?'

Sarah wasn't sure what to say, knowing that the truth would bring questions she wasn't ready to answer— the fact that Ren had purposely mislead her as to his true identity. She groaned as she recalled the things she'd said about the professor—about Ren, she corrected herself. He'd simply smiled and nodded. But why?

Again she tried to sit and this time was successful. 'I'm feeling fine now, Kevin. Thanks for scooping me up off the floor.' She forced a grin. 'I must have looked a sight!'

'You haven't answered my question. What caused you to faint?'

'Probably overworking myself. I've had quite a few emergencies this week and they've obviously taken their toll. I'll be fine. Thank you.' She straightened her shirt and retucked it into the band of her trousers. 'If you'll excuse me, I have a patient in day surgery who will refuse to have her operation unless I'm present so I'd better go before she yells the hospital down.' She held out a hand to Kevin. 'Thanks again.'

'No problem. Just slow down.'

'Yes, Doctor,' she said with a smile as she walked out of the treatment room. Her assumption had been correct. Bertie was arguing with one of the nurses who was asking her to change into a hospital operating gown.

'Not until me doctor gets here. I'll be doin' nuthin' that ya say.'

'Bertie,' Sarah's tone was reprimanding. 'I thought I told you to be nice to the staff.'

'Don't have ta do everythin' ya say, girlie,' Bertie snapped back, but Sarah could tell that she was pleased to see her. 'Where have ya been, anyway?' The scowl on her face was enough to terrify the nurse into leaving the room and Sarah began to help Bertie into her gown.

'I just went to check on my other patients. Ruby and Margaret are coming along fine and should be discharged later this week.'

'And Hilda?' The question was asked quietly as— although Hilda Birch and Bertie MacPhail hadn't always seen eye to eye during their lives—they still cared about each other.

'She underwent a bypass operation yesterday and appears to be on the way to a full recovery.'

'Good,' was the reply as she smacked one of Sarah's hands. 'I can dress meself, ya interferin' do-gooder.'

Sarah stood back and let her do so and after she'd struggled for a while with the ties at the rear of the gown, Sarah tut-tutted and was allowed to help.

'Pity your Dr Taylor couldn't come down as well.

Would have been more of a comfort ta me ta know you were both there while I'm under the knife.'

'You're not going under a knife—you're going under a laser,' Sarah corrected. 'And besides,' she said, clenching her jaw in anger, 'Dr Taylor's on holiday so the last place he'd want to come back to is this hospital.' Sarah tied the last tie on the gown so tightly that it broke off.

'Now look what ya've done, ya silly girl.'

'I'll get you another one.' Sarah slipped out of the room and requested another gown.

'Shredded the last one, did she?' the nurse asked and Sarah smiled.

'Her bark is a lot worse than her bite.' She returned to the room and this time Bertie didn't object to her help in dressing. Sarah was seething inside with anger. Her initial shock and disbelief had been swept aside. When they finally returned that evening she was going to give Ren Taylor—or, more to the point, Professor Fox-Taylor—a good piece of her mind. Then she was going to take great relish in throwing him and his belongings out of her house—whether he had some other place to sleep or not.

Lies, it was all lies. What else had he told her that was a lie? And only last night, she'd been stupid enough to confess her love for him. He'd mumbled something about her not understanding and she wondered if he was regretting his initial deceit. If that was the case she was going to make him regret it even more.

Bertie's operation proceeded with little fuss, which surprised Sarah. She thought that the old woman would fight tooth and nail with the surgeon—especially as she was awake for the entire procedure.

Sarah had observed with interest the techniques used

by Dr Anderson. Ophthalmology had never been one
of her strongest subjects but it was an honour to see
such an esteemed surgeon at work. The laser surgery
would reduce the pressure of the aqueous humour, sup-
posedly by stretching the drainage channels, which
would promote easier drainage. The reduction in pressure, by at least one third, would prevent further loss
of vision.

They wheeled the patient back to her room and Sarah
sat down beside the bed. 'That wasn't so bad, was it?'

'You ain't on this side, girlie.'

'Just rest now. They won't let you go home unless
you're completely rested and show all the natural
healthy symptoms.'

Bertie reached out an arthritic hand to Sarah, which
she took immediately. 'Don't ya tell anyone I said this
but thanks for stickin' by me. You've done ya
father proud.'

'It was my pleasure,' Sarah said, tears pricking in
her eyes. She knew how hard it was for Bertie to say
such emotional things and leaned forward to kiss the
older woman's forehead.

'Get away with ya,' she grumbled.

'If you insist,' Sarah replied, and stood up. 'I'll go
and check on Mike and be right back.' Making her way
to the orthopaedic wards, she realised that these were
Ren's wards. He was in charge of all of them and
held overall responsibility for the patients admitted to
them—regardless of who the surgeon was.

Mixed emotions flowed through her as she made her
way to Mike's room. She was proud of Ren for all that
he'd accomplished. Proud that the man she loved was
a success in his chosen field. She was also livid with
anger at his deception. All the stories she'd heard about

him were apparently true. He was ruthless, conceited, devious and, of course—her favourite adjective to describe him—arrogant.

How could she have fallen for such a man? Her father had always told her that initial impressions were often correct. Why hadn't she stuck with her initial impression of Ren? It had obviously been the right one.

She stood outside Mike's room and counted to twenty, trying to calm herself down before seeing her patient.

'Feeling any better?' she asked as she entered and stood by his bed.

'Much. Thanks again for all your help, Doc, and please thank Doc Taylor for me as well. One of the nurses here, not a bad looker either, said that he'd be back at the hospital soon and would be caring for me himself. She sounded surprised and when I asked her why—I really only did that to hear her sweet voice—' he grinned sheepishly '—she told me that I was considered a public patient and that the professor never monitored them: his registrars did.'

Sarah nodded but Mike continued with his story. 'I was more than a little confused when she told me that Doc Taylor was really Professor Fox-Taylor and was the big chief here. Can you believe it? She sounded almost scared of him and told me that a lot of the staff don't like him. So I told her that he was really a great bloke and a lot of fun. She looked at me like I had two heads, Doc. Weird, isn't it?'

'It's certainly that—and a lot more.' She mumbled the last part to herself.

'Did you know all the time? That he was the big cheese, I mean.'

'No. I only found out today.' Sarah glanced at her

watch, eager to have this conversation terminated. 'Listen, I've got to go and collect Bertie. . .'

'Oh, yeah, how did her op go?'

'Fine. She didn't threaten the surgeon at all.' They both grinned. 'Anyway, I've got to collect her and arrange to meet Trevor. You take care now and don't go chatting up too many nurses,' she told him sternly as she walked to the door. 'I'll probably be back this way in a few weeks but the hospital will send me regular updates on your condition. If there's anything you want, or if you need to get a message through to me, just ask one of the staff.'

'Right you are, Doc, and thanks again.'

It was another hour and a half before they were ready to discharge Bertie and even then they only relented because Sarah was with her. A taxi had been arranged to return them to the airport where they found Trevor, waiting for them.

Sarah looked at him and noticed a crumb of pastry at the corner of his mouth. She reached out a hand and brushed it away. 'Really, Trevor, if you're going to eat the pastries with the hope of not getting caught you must dispose of *all* the evidence.'

He grinned back at her and swiped a hand around his mouth and chin. 'Better?' he asked, and Sarah nodded. 'How'd you go, Bertie? Is the hospital still standing?'

'Watch ya mouth, Trevor Ross, or I'll be telling that sweet wife of yours all about them pastries.'

Trevor had the grace to colour and Bertie chuckled. 'Glad we understand each other. Let's get this plane off the ground and get me back 'ome.'

'Yes, ma'am.' Trevor saluted and soon they were up, up and away.

* * *

Sarah was still unsure how she was going to handle the situation with Ren when Trevor dropped her off. Bertie was staying the night with Edith and Trevor as she felt that she'd be 'in the way' at Sarah's house.

Sarah walked up the back steps, carrying their evening meal. The way she was feeling now she would rather throw the food at him but refused to waste good cooking. He was in the kitchen, waiting for the kettle to boil, when she entered the room and placed the food on the table.

'Hi,' he said, and Sarah could only nod. 'How did it all go?'

'Fine.' She stared at him for a moment, her heart doing somersaults at the sight of him. Why, oh, why, did he affect her in such a way? 'I think I'll have a shower.' She turned and walked out of the door but he caught up with her in the hallway.

'Sarah. . .we need to talk. Please come back and sit down.' He clasped one hand around her arm.

She stood with her back to him, trying hard to control her breathing. The temptation to simply turn around and connect one hand with his cheek was almost too much to resist. . .but resist she did. Instead she said icily, 'Please take your hands off me.'

He removed his hands as though she'd physically burnt him. She turned and walked back into the kitchen, sat at the table and folded her arms across her chest in self-defence.

'Are you sure everything went OK today?' He sat down opposite her.

'Perfectly. Mike sends his thanks for everything you did for him. Dr Anderson sends his best regards. . .oh, and so does Kevin.'

'That's nice,' he said warily. They were silent for a

moment before Ren took a deep breath and said, 'About last night, Sarah. I'm terribly sorry I lost my temper.'

'I wouldn't worry about it, Ren. From what I can gather you've done a very commendable job of controlling it the entire time you've been here.'

'Pardon?' His brow furrowed in confusion.

'Your temper. Although you don't yell or throw things most of your staff don't seem to like you very much.' She raised a finger thoughtfully to her chin. 'Maybe it's not your temper, as such, but your general disregard for anyone's feelings. Yes, maybe that's your main problem, *Professor*.' She recrossed her arms and glared at him.

His Adam's apple seemed to work overtime as he swallowed a few times, before leaning back in his chair. 'How did you find out?'

Sarah stood up and banged her fists onto the table. 'That's not the question, Ren—or should I call you Lawrence? The question is why didn't you tell me in the first place. I shouldn't have had to find out from anyone. I know you have a hard time trusting people but not to confess your true identity is stretching things a little too far, don't you think?' She began pacing across the room as her anger demanded action.

'You really had me fooled. . .the whole town, in fact. Are you congratulating yourself on your little deception? Didn't you think such a small country town could cope with the fact of having a famous surgeon in its midst? How dare you treat this community in such an appalling manner? Are we all so lower class that you couldn't reveal your true identity? Country hicks don't mix with English aristocracy, do they?

'You are *the* most overbearing, egotistical, hypocritical, lying, chauvinistic. . .'

'Don't forget arrogant,' he supplied.

'I was leaving that for last, but you are. You are the most. . .'

'Not again—you've just said that line,' he had the nerve to point out, a huge grin splitting his face.

'Don't you dare look cute and appealing because I won't fall for it this time, do you understand me? I might have thought myself in love with you but I could never, *never*,' she said vehemently, 'allow myself to fall in love with a man like you. It goes against all my principles.'

'Sarah.' He stood and came across to her, clasping a hand firmly onto each arm to halt her pacing. 'Sarah, let me defend myself.'

'It's too late, Ren.' She broke free from his grasp. 'There is no explanation you could give me that could redeem you. I want you packed and out of my house this instant, and this time I mean it—even if I have to throw you out myself.'

He had the audacity to chuckle. 'I'd like to see that.'

'How dare you patronise me!' she said, her eyes blazing with anger, and this time gave in to the temptation to strike her hand across his cheek. 'Get out!' She turned on her heel and stormed out of the house. Whistling for Sebastian, she vaulted onto him, grabbed a handful of his mane and galloped off. Away from the house. Away from Ren.

On and on she rode, letting Sebastian pick the route they should take. They knew this land so well that, regardless of her temper, there was no chance of them getting lost. The cool breeze on her face was working miracles and when she reached one of her favourite spots she slowed the stallion down, before dismounting.

Burying her face against her horse, she sobbed her

heart out. The pain and anguish she'd suppressed for most of the day came to the fore and overflowed like a waterfall. 'How could he?' she asked her bewildered horse who kept nuzzling his mistress, trying to comfort her.

She finally stopped crying and sat down beneath a tree to watch the sun set and the stars appear—one by one. As a child she had often sat and waited for the first star of the night to appear and each time she'd made her secret wish. Tonight was no different, although it seemed impossible that her wish could ever come true—that Ren was simply an ordinary man who never lied, who trusted and who loved her as much as she loved him.

She had no idea how long she'd sat there and eventually—when every emotion felt as though it had been wrenched from her body and soul—she stood and remounted Sebastian.

'Thanks for always been there for me,' she told her horse as she lovingly stroked his neck. 'Let's go home.' They set off in the dark of night at an easy gallop. They hadn't gone far when she saw Sebastian's ears prick up and Sarah felt an overwhelming sense of danger.

Suddenly he reared and Sarah groped for another handful of mane while she tried to quieten him down. Her words were having no affect on him and she presumed that a snake had spooked him. He reared again and this time Sarah was jolted backwards off Sebastian—to land on the ground with a heavy thud, her head connecting with something hard.

'Ouch,' she cried before the darkness enveloped her.

Sarah's head began to pound with pain as a bright light was shone on her face. Was she travelling toward the bright light she'd heard so many people talk about?

'Over here,' she heard a masculine voice call as branches and leaves were crunched under heavy footfalls.

'Trevor, over here.' The voice was urgent now and she vaguely recognised it as belonging to Ren. 'Sarah? Sarah, can you hear me?'

She found that her brain was too fuzzy and her mouth too dry to bother with speech. Trying to open her eyes, Sarah's head was once again pierced with pain and she gave up in defeat. It was too hard.

'Oh, Sarah, my love. Thank God we found you.' A warm hand brushed over her face in a caress. Slowly all other sounds faded into an incoherent mumble and Sarah slipped back into the darkness that held no pain.

The next time she woke she felt as though she were floating in mid-air. The ground beneath her had turned from cold, solid dirt to a bed of feathers—all snug and warm. She sighed, enjoying the sensation of weightlessness before drifting off to fly to a new place in time.

Sarah was bathed in sweat yet her mouth felt dry and choked with fear as she felt herself falling—spiralling down and out of control. Faster and faster she spun, her arms flung out wide trying to grasp something—anything—on her way down. She must try harder. If she didn't succeed in finding something to hold onto she would hit the ground with such an impact that she would shatter into a thousand pieces.

Thankfully her hand finally grasped something solid. It was someone else's hand and she looked up, suspended in mid-air. It was Ren.

'Don't let me go!' she cried, but could already feel his grip starting to loosen. 'Ren!' she screamed. 'Don't let me go—*please hold onto me.*'

'I will, Sarah, I'll never let you go.' At his words the panic drained from her and the pleasant floating sensation returned. She was safe—she was with Ren.

Sunlight peeped through her bedroom curtains and Sarah slowly opened her eyes. Her head was pounding with an enormous headache and she wondered what she had been doing to receive such punishment.

Throwing back the bed covers, she went to lift her legs over the side of the bed when Edith quickly began to cover her up again.

'Shh, Sarah. Lie still and rest.'

'Edith? What are you doing here?' Her throat was very scratchy and Edith immediately held out a glass of water for her to sip from.

'Ren gave us strict orders to keep you in bed.'

'Ren? I thought he'd left. Where is he, anyway?'

'He's gone out to see Lizzie and young Reuben.'

'How dare he! They're my patients. The man has got to stop interfering in my life.' Again Sarah tried to get out of bed but Edith pushed her back with more force.

'You're in no condition to do anything except lie there, Sarah Rutherford. You should be grateful to Ren for the help he's given you. Now you do as you're told and stay in bed until the doctor returns—or you'll have me to answer to,' Edith said in her best no-nonsense tone.

Sarah relented and rested back against the pillows. 'What time is it?'

'It's after ten. Are you hungry at all?'

'Not really.'

'In any pain? Ren left some tablets here for you to take, if necessary.'

'No,' she replied hesitantly. 'No, I'm not in a great deal of pain—just a headache.' Sarah frowned. 'Boy, did I have some terrible dreams last night.'

'I'm not surprised,' Edith chuckled and settled herself down in the chair beside the bed.

'What do you mean?'

'Ren says you have mild concussion. Don't you remember what happened?' Edith asked slowly and Sarah shook her head, groaning as she did so. 'You were thrown off Sebastian and hit your head on a log. We were all frantic with worry when Sebastian returned home without you.'

Sarah raised a hand to her head, a look of amazement on her face. 'I remember going out for a ride but that's all.'

'Do you remember *why* you went out for a ride?'

'Yes. Yes, I do. I was angry with Ren.'

'Do you remember why you were angry with him?'

'Yes,' Sarah said softly, and the feelings of heartache came crashing down upon her. 'He lied to me, Edith. Why would he do such a thing?'

'He told us about his position of Professor at the hospital and that you'd felt deceived by him.'

'Did he explain why?' Sarah asked, tears beginning to flood her eyes.

'No, missy, he didn't. But he did ask us to trust him.'

'Trust.' She laughed bitterly as she wiped the tears away. 'That's what he said to me but I don't see him doing any trusting, considering that he felt it necessary to lie to me.'

'Be patient, love.' Edith placed her hand in Sarah's and gave it a little squeeze. 'I'm sure he has his reasons.'

'Well, they'd better be good.' Sarah's bottom lip began to wobble and fresh tears began to flow. 'It's hopeless, Edith,' she wailed, clinging tightly to the other woman's hand. 'I love him. I love him so very much.'

'I know, missy. I know,' Edith soothed.

Sarah was dozing when Ren put his head around the door but she could sense that he was there. She pretended to be sleeping when he walked over to the bed and picked up her wrist to take her pulse. His eyes seemed to bore into her and she could feel herself beginning to blush.

'Faker,' he accused softly as he lowered her wrist. 'I know you're awake, Sarah.'

'Good, then go away,' she mumbled as she turned her back to him.

'That's no way to speak to your doctor.'

'You're *not* my doctor,' she replied fiercely, wishing that he would go away and leave her alone.

'I beg to differ, considering that I'm the one who's been prescribing your medication.'

That got her attention and she turned swiftly to look at him. The action caused her head to pound and she groaned with pain.

'Still a bit sore? You will be for at least another week. That was quite a knock you gave yourself.' When she didn't reply he asked, 'Would you like some more codeine?'

'No. . .thank you.' She forced herself to be polite. 'I understand you've been seeing my patients again.'

'You were in no condition to perform Lizzie's check-up . . . ' he shrugged '. . .so I guessed it was up to me. Now, the doctor's orders for the remainder of the day are complete bed-rest, no loud music, no reading, no television. . .oh, and no speaking.' He grinned down at her and Sarah clenched her hands into fists.

'Oh, OK, I'll relent on the last one. You can talk if you wish.'

'Thank you,' she replied caustically.

He waved a hand in her direction. 'Don't mention it.' He'd wheeled in her portable sphygmomanometer and was reaching for the cuff. She waited patiently while he took her blood pressure and gave him an ironical smile when he announced that it was back to normal.

'I'll just check your pupils,' he said in his best 'doctor' tone and picked up the ophthalmoscope that was on her bedside table. Odd that she hadn't noticed the instruments lying around before. She obeyed his instructions on where to look, knowing that internal bleeding inside the brain could first be detected by enlargement of the pupils.

'Anything else, *Doctor*?' she asked sweetly.

'Only this.' He quickly bent his head and brushed his lips across hers. 'Now rest,' he said as he walked to the door. 'I'll be back to see you later.'

Sarah breathed a sigh of relief as he shut the door behind him. The contact between them—that brief kiss—had stirred to life all the emotions she was trying so hard to quell. Her body had felt warmed at his touch, then cold at its briefness. None of her feelings had diminished—not one iota—instead they had increased.

'Damn you, Ren Taylor,' she said and turned her face into the pillow.

CHAPTER TEN

SARAH dozed on and off for the remainder of the day and blatantly tried her hardest to ignore Ren when he came in to do her observations. Edith had brought in food but Sarah only picked at it, putting her lack of appetite down to her emotional turmoil over Ren rather than her concussion.

She woke again and noticed that it was dark outside. Sighing, she snuggled deeper under the covers. Tasmania was known for its cooler-than-usual nights and it seemed that tonight was no exception.

The feel of a pleasant heat, radiating down through her tired and aching shoulder and neck muscles, made Sarah groan in delight. Rousing herself from her sleep, she realised that Ren was giving her a massage. She rolled onto her stomach to ensure that every bit of her shoulders received attention.

'Mmm, wonderful.' The massage continued, causing Sarah to remain in her half dozing state.

'You're so tense, Sarah. You must relax or your headaches will get worse.'

She frowned. 'Don't speak to me as a doctor, Ren. If you are, you may as well not say anything at all.' His hands stilled for a moment and her frown increased. 'That doesn't mean you have to stop massaging me.'

He chuckled and resumed the rhythmic massage. 'I wonder. . .' he said, his voice so deep and smooth that Sarah relaxed a little more. 'Are you this tense from your fall or from your discovery about me?'

'About you,' she replied dreamily.

'How do you come to that conclusion?'

'I've had many falls from a horse in my time and I've had mild concussion before. My muscles were never this tense so it means that the blame lies on the extenuating circumstances.'

'I guess you're right.'

She could feel her muscles turning to jelly under his skilful technique and the tension draining out of her.

'Why didn't you tell me the truth?' she asked, her voice heavy and drugged with sleep.

He was silent for a few minutes. 'There's more to all of this than meets the eye. I still can't tell you why I felt it necessary to deceive you but it is definitely not what you think. I've come to care about the people of this community in a very short time, especially you. Believe me, Sarah, I'd been trying to figure out a way to come clean but knew it would be futile until I could return to Hobart. All I can do now is to ask you to trust me. . .for just a little while longer.' His voice was hypnotic but one part of Sarah's brain was still functioning.

'I don't know if I can any more.'

'Please try. You've come to mean so much to me. . .'

'How much?' she interrupted, not wanting to discuss his deception any longer.

'More than I can express with words,' he said softly. Slowly he pulled up the T-shirt she slept in higher so that his fingers could connect properly with her skin. His massage began to emcompass the rest of her back—rubbing and soothing her beyond belief.

Her body began to tingle as Ren brought her senses to life, and for some inexplicable reason Sarah no longer felt like sleeping.

'If I recall correctly,' he whispered, his mouth quite close to her ear, 'I owe you a massage.' His teeth nipped her earlobe and Sarah gasped. Her hands were clenched into fists again but this time it was for an entirely different reason.

His fingers seemed to know exactly where to go and how to evoke the required response from her. Sarah stopped fighting it and forced herself to consciously relax, her fingers spread wide in the effort.

'Good idea,' he breathed down her neck as his lips connected with her skin in a row of tiny kisses. His hands encompassed the side of her rib cage, brushing her breasts lightly. All Sarah's relaxation techniques went out of the window and she jumped at the contact.

His answering chuckle was almost euphoric at her reaction to his touch. He reached for her arm and began to turn her onto her back. 'Sarah. . .' he whispered into the darkened room. 'Oh, Sarah.'

His lips found hers with an urgency that she matched. Her fingers entwined themselves in his hair, holding his head firmly in place. This was where she wanted to be—where she belonged. Her feelings for Ren would never die. She knew that now and let the love flow freely from her.

Their tongues meshed in hungry unison as though they'd both been deprived of intimacy for eternity. Passion flared between them as Ren slowly eased himself onto the bed beside her, his arms clamped firmly around her—moulding her to fit his body perfectly.

Sarah reluctantly broke free from his mouth, gasping in air as though her lungs were about to burst. She noted with satisfaction that his breathing was as ragged as hers as they clung to each other.

'Sorry,' she said hesitantly, her head buried in his

chest. 'I thought I might die from too much ecstasy if I didn't come up for air.'

'We certainly set each other on fire, don't we?'

'I've never felt like this with anyone before,' she confessed.

'Nor I,' he admitted, and Sarah's heart rejoiced. Maybe. . .just maybe there was a ray of hope for them.

'Ren. . .' Sarah spoke hesitantly after a few minutes had passed. 'Do you want to. . .?'

He kissed the top of her head and tightened his hold on her. 'You're in no condition to do anything except sleep. Close your eyes, Sarah.'

'You're sounding like a doctor again.'

'It's just as well.' He breathed in deeply, held it for a few moments and then slowly exhaled. 'It's just as well,' he repeated.

Sarah snuggled in closer, relishing the feel of him and how safe and secure she felt in his arms. Tomorrow they would talk and if necessary she would go with him to Hobart to find out exactly what it was that was keeping them apart. Tomorrow everything would be fixed.

Tomorrow everything was not fixed. In fact, it was at least a hundred times worse than it had been when she'd gone to sleep in Ren's arms.

He had gone without a word. No goodbye. He'd left and returned to Hobart.

Sarah had woken to find herself snuggled against her pillow and for a moment or two had wondered whether the previous night's events had been a dream. 'Nah,' she told herself and slowly levered herself out of bed.

Every muscle in her body ached but her head pounded. She reached for the codeine tablets beside the bed and swallowed them, before attempting to do anything else.

It was cool and she knew that she should put her robe on if she didn't want to catch a cold on top of everything else, but she didn't have the energy to perform the simple task. Wandering into the kitchen, Sarah had expected to breathe in the smell of freshly brewed coffee but didn't, as it hadn't been made. Going through the motions, she sat down at the table and waited.

The next thing she noticed was how quiet her house was. She had expected to hear the shower running, or sounds coming from Ren's room, but there was nothing. She rose and shuffled around the house, checking every room. His bedroom was the last one, as though her heart was telling her not to look there first because all evidence of Ren Taylor's presence in her home would have miraculously disappeared.

The room was bare, the bed stripped. He was gone.

Sarah made her way back to the kitchen, refusing to believe the evidence that was before her very eyes. Maybe he'd gone to see Lizzie—and taken his luggage with him? Perhaps he'd taken her threat of two days ago seriously and had cleared out—but why now? He'd never done as she'd asked before. It didn't make any sense.

She drank three cups of coffee and still came up with no answers. Deciding that as Edith always knew what was going on within the community, she'd give her a call.

'Are you all right, missy?' Edith asked, after picking up the phone on the first ring. She hadn't even said hello, as though she knew that it would be Sarah calling and why.

'Of course I'm all right. Why shouldn't I be?' Sarah

snapped, and instantly regretted her words. 'Sorry. I guess I'm still a little concussed—I'd never speak to you like that, otherwise.'

Edith tried to laugh but didn't succeed. 'I'll be right over. You stay put until I get there.'

'Edith,' Sarah said firmly before they were disconnected, 'where is he?' She knew the answer without being told, but needed to hear it anyway.

'He left for Hobart early this morning. A private plane came, collected him and whisked him away. I'm sorry, missy. But I'm sure he'll be back,' Edith added, although even her usually cheerful tone belied her words.

'He's not coming back,' Sarah said glumly. 'He's gone.'

He left on a Wednesday, eleven days after he'd burst into her life and changed her for ever. Sarah knew that work was her only hope of survival. Even though the theatre was scrubbed and ready for an emergency, Sarah rescrubbed the entire theatre—to expend her pent-up energy.

Her clinic that Wednesday afternoon was larger than usual, owing to her cancelled clinic on Monday. There were mainly minor ailment complaints and Sarah was thankful not to be faced with emotional patients. Being a GP, she often had to play the role of psychologist— to help the mental status of her patients before they would allow their bodies to heal.

Edith brought her lunch over and stayed to eat with her. 'Now that Bertie's settled back into her home I got lonely so I decided to come and eat with you today.'

Sarah gave her a rueful smile. 'It's OK. I know what

you're doing and I appreciate it, but I'll have to get
over him sooner or later.'

'Why?'

'What do you mean—why? He left—without
a word.'

'Why don't you go to Hobart and confront him?'

'Because if he'd wanted to see me again I'm sure he
would have waited to say goodbye and arranged a time
to meet. Instead he sneaks out, like a thief, and
leaves me.'

'What about that prototype you've been working on?
Hasn't Ren taken it with him?'

Sarah clapped a hand to her mouth. 'Oh, Edith, you're
right. I'd totally forgotten about it.' Sarah jumped up
from the table and raced to her office. The design specifications were still there, but the device wasn't. She
returned to the kitchen, her face pale. 'What am I going
to do now?'

'I'm not sure I understand. What's the problem?'

'It's not patented. Ren could quite easily make some
minor adjustments and claim it as his own.'

Edith shook her head. 'He wouldn't do that.'

'How do you know? The man whisks in and out of
our lives—deceiving us the entire time he's here—and
you want to trust him? Go ahead.'

'That's not the impression I received.' Edith seemed
to be choosing her words carefully. 'If what you say is
true, regarding his staff and colleagues not liking him
very much, then maybe coming here and being an
anonymous person enabled Ren to be himself. The *real*
him, as we'd no previous acquaintance to pre-judge him
on. I'm not usually wrong about people I meet and I
can tell straight off the bat whether they're decent sorts.

I liked Ren. . .I still do and I'm sure he has a very good reason for acting the way he is.'

Sarah shook her head. 'I don't know how you can trust him so easily.'

'I have no other choice. . .' Edith shrugged '. . .and neither do you. Didn't he want to perform some tests on your device?'

'That's what he said but. . .'

'Then maybe that's exactly what he's doing. Give it time, Sarah. He'll contact you, I'm sure of it.'

Sarah felt a little better when Edith left and, upon rethinking their conversations regarding the prototype, she hoped that her friend was right. After all, it was the professor she'd been trying to contact the entire time and, unbeknownst to her, he'd been right under her nose, giving her the feedback she'd been hoping for.

The fact that he alone held the power to decide the future of her device was an alarming fact, but Sarah had come to that conclusion when she'd first decided to pursue him. She heard the door open and close, announcing her next patient. She put all thoughts of Ren Taylor aside which, under the circumstances, wasn't at all easy.

On Friday Ruby Maddox returned from Hobart and Sarah drove over to check on her post-operative care.

'Ruby, I want you to let Bill do all the running around. You're to take it easy for at least another week. Understand?' Sarah asked in her strictest voice.

'But I don't want to make any extra work for my Bill. He's not that good at housework or cooking and to see him fret over it would make me worse, Doctor.'

'That's all been taken care of, Ruby. The women have organised a roster for meals, as well as helping

around the house for the next week. After that we'll
see how you're going and, if necessary, we'll organise
yet another week of support.'

'But it's not fair on the other ladies.'

'You've helped other families when they've been in
need and now it's your turn. Your recovery depends
entirely on your attitude. If you follow my orders and
do as you're told then it should only be for the week.
If you get out of bed too often and fuss around then it
will be longer. I've spoken to Bill and he's willing to
do anything to help you get better.' Sarah stood at the
end of Ruby's bed with her hands planted firmly on
her hips, waiting for the decision.

'All right, Doctor. I'll do as you ask.'

'I knew I could count on you.' Sarah smiled and
relaxed her severe pose. Ruby returned the smile and
shook her head.

'You're a real softie beneath that professional
exterior, Sarah Rutherford. Did I tell you that Dr Taylor
stopped by to see me this morning before I was transferred?'

'Oh. . .did he?' Sarah tried to keep her voice light
and uninterested.

'Yes,' Ruby glowed. 'He's such a wonderful man
and so highly regarded in the hospital. I was amazed
when the nurse came in and told me who he really was.
She seemed rather flustered at his visit but he was so
charming and caring. I couldn't thank him enough for
everything he'd done for me and my Bill.'

Sarah thought she was going to gag on the gushing
sentimentality over the wonderful Dr Taylor. 'That's
great, Ruby. I'm glad he stopped by to see you. Now,
I'd better be getting over to see Bertie and check that
she's behaving herself.'

Sarah was detained another ten minutes, answering questions regarding Bertie's health, young Mike Jayton and, of course, her good friend Hilda Birch. She'd gone through the routine with many of her other patients when they'd come to the clinic. The community cared—no one could ever accuse them of less—but sometimes Sarah felt as though she were the source of gossip and updates. Maybe she should print a brochure and circulate it—at least that way she wouldn't have to hear about the wonderful Dr Taylor from everyone she met!

Thankfully she finally made her way out of the Maddox household and drove to Bertie's, eager to have a no-nonsense conversation with her good friend.

'So. . .can ya survive without 'im?' was the first thing Bertie said to her as she walked in the door. Sarah was tempted to turn around and walk directly out again but forced herself to keep moving forward.

'Ya've gotta chase after 'im, ya silly girl. That's what all us womenfolk 'ave ta do if we wanna catch our man. I had ta do it, ya mother had ta do it and even Edith Ross had ta do it.'

'It's not that simple,' Sarah said, and put in the anaesthetic drops. She reached for her ophthalmoscope, while waiting for the anaesthetic to take affect. 'Have you been putting your drops in?'

'Nah,' Bertie grumbled. 'What do ya reckon? Of course I've been puttin' them in.'

'Just checking. . .in case senility finally sets in.'

'Ya watch ya mouth, girlie.' Bertie swiped a hand at her backside, but Sarah neatly sidestepped it.

'It it weren't for ya. . .'

'Yeah, yeah, I know,' Sarah mumbled, and pulled out her Perkins tonometer.

'I hear Ruby's back from Hobart,' Bertie said and the inquisition began all over again.

Sarah closed up her bag. 'Right, that's it. I'll be back in a few days time. Call me if you have any problems.'

'I don't need ta call ya. I've got a different woman droppin' 'round every day, and ya can be sure that if there was anythin' wrong they'd be over ta ya surgery so fast ta tell ya that old Bertie's finally losin' it.'

Sarah smiled. 'That'll be the day.' She leaned over and gave Bertie a kiss on the cheek and the older woman grabbed her in a rough hug. Sarah was so startled that she almost cried at the intimacy.

'Don't ya worry, lovey,' she said softly. 'It'll work itself out. He'll come round.'

Sarah pulled back and looked at the woman who'd once scared most of the town's population away from her. 'Thanks,' she sniffed.

'Ah, get away with ya.' Bertie gently shoved her backwards. 'And don't ya go tellin' anyone that I was. . .well, ya know. It's just that I do love ya, girlie, and I hate ta see ya hurtin'.'

Sarah was too choked up with emotion to speak. Instead she reached for her bag, said goodbye and quickly got into her car.

Sarah continued to drag herself out of bed every morning and go through her daily routine. Seeing her patients, running her clinics, eating, breathing, sleeping. Anything and everything to try and forget her heartache.

On Monday Margaret Braithwaite came home and Sarah proceeded with her post-operative regime. On Tuesday she sat down and filled in the necessary paperwork to request a district nurse for the area. After all, one could only try.

On Wednesday she paid her final morning visit to Lizzie Dumar and baby Reuben. Lizzie's mother had arrived safely and the whole family seemed a lot happier. Lizzie's next check-up would be in another four weeks.

On Thursday she received a fax—the letterhead denoting it came from the office of Professor L.M.S. Fox-Taylor. An appointment had been made for Dr Sarah Rutherford to speak with the professor the following day with regard to her prototype.

Sarah scrunched the fax into a tight little ball and threw it against the wall—at least half a dozen times. She was expected to simply drop everything she was doing and go to Hobart. Obviously Ren didn't think that her practice or her patients were as important as he was. Angry and annoyed as she was, she knew she'd go.

She had only five patients booked in for a clinic on Friday and it was no trouble to reschedule them to her Monday clinic. She had no home visits booked for the weekend and decided that she'd go to Hobart, hear what the man had to say and then visit some of her old friends.

She faxed a reply, indicating that—after juggling and reshuffling her schedule—she'd be able to attend the appointment with His Royal Highness, the Professor. She didn't care what his secretary thought about her reference to Ren and sincerely hoped that she'd show it to him.

He still seemed to have no regard for other people's feelings, nor did he seem to care that people went out of their way just for him. She called Edith and told her of her plans. Naturally Edith sounded excited and her first question was, 'What are you going to wear?'

Truthfully Sarah hadn't given it a lot of thought and,

considering Ren had seen her in everything from her
jeans to her night attire—and less—she didn't think
that the question was relevant.

'But you must, Sarah,' Edith persisted when Sarah
relayed her feelings. 'You must knock his socks off and
leave him begging for you. Why don't you drive down
tonight and go shopping tomorrow morning before your
appointment?' Edith suggested.

Sarah mulled this idea over. 'I'll think about it.'

Sarah was almost disgusted with herself when she did
exactly as Edith had suggested. She had been browsing
in some of Hobart's finer clothes shops since they'd
opened that morning. Her appointment with the
professor wasn't until three-thirty that afternoon so she
had some time to kill.

She'd already bought a new pair of jeans, a few tops
and three pairs of shoes. For this afternoon she knew
that a business suit would be more suitable than a flirty
dress. She smiled to herself as she entered yet another
shop. How would Ren react if she waltzed in, dressed
to the nines, and threw herself on his desk? Would he
politely offer her a chair? Or would he ravish her?

She shook her head at her childish musings, and
began to look at some elegant and well-cut suits, thankful that fashion allowed her to look every inch the
professional that she was—yet still remain sexy and
very much a woman.

Sarah tried on several suits and in the end was caught
between one of deep russet red and one of black. The
black suit had satin lapels on the jacket, giving it a
formal air. She decided, for this particular purpose, to
go with the russet red as it highlighted her brown eyes.

Satisfied with her purchases, she made an appointment to have her hair done. If she wanted to knock Ren's socks off she may as well go through the entire process. She had lunch at Café Lella's, realising belatedly that she might bump into Ren, but good fortune was on her side and she ate her fill of goodies before she walked to the hospital to change.

In the basement toilets she transformed herself into Dr Sarah Rutherford, MBBS. Fellow of the Royal Australasian College of General Practitioners. She applied her make-up carefully, and when she was done gave herself a satisfied smile.

She wanted to portray to Ren a 'look but don't touch' image, knowing that it would drive him wild. He'd already confessed that he found her attractive and she was hoping that this outfit would tip the scales, giving her the upper hand. She'd borrowed a friend's locker and once her other clothes were safely tucked away she made her way to the wards.

'Wow,' Mike said as she strolled through the door. 'Doc? Is that you?' He tried to sit up a little straighter in bed but the traction prevented him from doing so. Sarah did a twirl in front of him.

'What do you think?'

'You scrub up real good, Doc.' His eyes widened appreciatively at the way the suit showed off her fabulous figure.

'Funny. . . Hilda Birch's reaction was almost the same as yours.' Sarah sat down beside his bed.

'How is she? And how's everyone else back home?' Poor Mike was terribly home sick and made it sound as though he'd left his family in a different country. She gave him up to-date progress reports on his fellow patients who had now been released from this 'prison' and also brought news of his family.

'Simon's arm is still in plaster and his cast is literally covered with drawings and signatures.'

'That's our Simon,' Mike beamed. 'And Dad's coping OK?'

'He's fine. Don't worry—only a few more weeks and you'll be out of here.'

'Yeah, that's what Doc Taylor said this morning.' He raised a hand to his forehead. 'I keep forgetting that I should really be calling him Professor Fox-Taylor but I can't. It doesn't seem to suit him.'

Sarah simply nodded at his statement, the butterflies in her stomach churning even more than they had previously. 'I have an appointment with him in about ten minutes so I guess I'd better go and find his office.'

'No need,' a deep voice said from behind her, and she turned in astonishment to look up at Ren. He looked magnificently handsome and very untouchable in his three-piece suit, with his white coat hanging loosely over the top. The very picture of English aristocracy, she thought.

'I'd be more than delighted to show you the way.' He waited for her to stand and Sarah cursed herself for wearing high heels. The moment she put weight on them, she was sure she was going to topple over and completely disgrace herself. She gave him another look and saw him wink at Mike. 'I'll be around to see you later this evening, Mike. Shall we go, Dr Rutherford?' He held out a hand and inclined his head toward the door, indicating that she should go first.

They walked along down the corridor, out of the wards and turned into yet another long corridor. Neither of them spoke. Sarah was trying hard to think of something polite and inconsequential to say to him but couldn't. His presence had so unnerved her that it was all she could do to concentrate on staying upright in these shoes.

The silence stretched on, and the only words Ren spoke were the ones giving her directions to his office. He gave his secretary a brief nod as he passed her and held the door for Sarah to precede him.

When it was firmly shut he leant against it for a brief moment and let his eyes slowly appraise her figure. 'You look fantastic!' His eyes held the intimacy she'd always wanted from him but Sarah hardened her heart. She was here about her prototype and was not going to let him sidetrack her.

'Do you mind if I sit down, or did you ask me here merely to ogle me?'

'I beg your pardon.' He inclined his head in a little bow again, that satisfied smirk on his face. So, he wanted her off guard—and he knew that he'd succeeded. 'Please forgive my manners, Dr Rutherford. Won't you sit down?' He indicated a chair opposite his desk, before seating himself in the comfortable leather chair which knew only his shape.

'I trust everyone is well? Edith, Trevor. . .'

'Everyone is fine,' she answered curtly.

'And you?' His voice softened and he gazed at her across the desk. 'How are you, Sarah?'

'Fine. Can we please get down to business?'

'Certainly.' He shuffled some papers into order and bent to pick up two boxes that were on the floor beside his desk. From the first box, he took out Sarah's prototype and handed her a set of documents.

'These are the results of the tests that I told you about. Every device that is to be considered for the medical market must go through rigorous testing before the FDA will even look at an application. As you will see, your device passed most of them. . .but not all.'

He opened the second box and brought out another device that looked almost identical to hers. Almost, but not quite. He handed it to her and she hesitantly took it. . .making sure that their hands did not make contact.

'What's this?' she asked, after turning it over a few times.

'That is *my* device. It performs the same function as yours, although there is one major difference between the two.'

Sarah was dumbfounded. He *had* stolen her idea. He had pulled her prototype to pieces and improved it where it had initially failed—and had the gall to call it *his*. She stood up and gently placed the device on his desk, wishing that she could throw it at his head.

'I think I've heard enough.' Tears began to gather in her eyes. 'This was the reason, wasn't it?' She pointed to his desk where the evidence lay guiltily before him. 'This was the reason you didn't tell me who you were. You knew from my various attempts to gain an appointment with you that I had something of value that *you* wanted. When you accidentally stumbled across me in the middle of nowhere you probably congratulated yourself on your good fortune.

'Tell me, Ren, was seducing me part of your plan or was that just an added bonus. . .the fact that you found me attractive?' She shook her head in disgust. 'The whole time we were together you kept telling me to trust you. Ha!' Her hands were balled into fists by her side, while feelings of dejection welled up inside her.

'Sarah. . .' He stood and reached out a hand to her.

'Don't you dare touch me. I knew you had a strong interest in my prototype and at first I was reluctant to tell you anything about it. But you looked at me with those hypnotic eyes and said, "Trust me, Sarah," and foolishly I did.' A single tear ran down her cheek and angrily she brushed it away.

'You'll ruin your make-up,' he said, and offered her a tissue.

'Don't try to be cute, Ren. I'm wise to your game and I no longer wish to play it.' She took a deep breath and pointed again to his desk. 'You can keep the device. Plagiarise it, throw it in the bin or use it as a paper weight. . .I no longer care.' She turned and almost ran out of his office.

'Sarah.' She heard him call after her but didn't turn back. Instead she ignored the astonished look his secretary gave her and continued on her way back to the basement. She ripped off the suit and kicked it into the corner. So much for appearing cool, calm and collected.

She scrubbed at her face and ran her fingers through her hair, before pulling on her jeans and shirt. She looked at herself in the mirror. A sad, despondent and lonely woman was reflected there. 'You gambled. . . and you lost.'

Picking up the suit, Sarah refolded it and put it back in the bag. The thought of returning it entered her mind, but she did like the outfit and it seemed silly to return it simply to spite Ren when she was sure that he'd never even know.

She walked out of the hospital and dumped her extra bags into her car. Coffee. That's what she needed. Coffee and something really, really sinful to eat. Her feet took her back to the coffee-shop she'd been in only a few hours ago and, sitting at her favourite table, Sarah ordered her remedy for a broken heart.

She was on her third Danish, her eyes downcast into

her coffee, when she realised that someone was standing beside her.

'May I sit down?' Sarah's entire body convulsed into life at hearing that voice. That deep, resonant, English aristocratic voice. There was nothing pompous or arrogant in his tone and she slowly raised her eyes to meet his.

He'd stripped off his white coat, suit jacket and waisteant. His tie was loosened and the top few buttons of his shirt were undone. His hair was almost sticking up on end, as though he'd been trying to pull it out. He looked more like her beloved Ren than ever before.

'May I sit down?' he asked again and Sarah waved a hand at the empty seat opposite her. A waitress came and took his order, then once again they were alone. 'Sarah, I beg you, *please* let me explain.' He remained silent while waiting for her nod. 'Thank you.' He reached out and took her hand to his—Sarah didn't have the strength to pull away. All her energy was gone.

'You've laid a few charges at my door and now I would like to defend myself and do it truthfully. Your initial impression of why I decided to stay at your home was correct. When I heard Mike mention a Dr Rutherford I began to wonder whether this was the same person who'd been trying to gain an appointment with me, although I had no idea what your business was about.' He looked a little sheepish when he said, 'To be honest, I was expecting a man.

'I'd finished fixing up that little boy after his incident with calf-dehorning when I saw the design specifications for your device on your desk. I realised that this was obviously what your business with me was about and, considering the evidence I laid before you in my office, it was imperative that I got a closer look at your prototype. That was the reason I decided to stay.'

'But why didn't you. . .?'

'Please.' He held up a hand. 'Let me say what I have to. Believe me, Sarah, this isn't easy for me.' Again he waited for her consenting nod and continued. 'I knew I should have come clean but I've never been able to trust people, as you well know, so I can only offer my natural suspicious nature as my defence.' Ren took a sip of his coffee, as though seeking added strength.

'My device has been through FDA and is at the manufacturers, getting ready for mass production.' Sarah sat up straighter in her chair and looked at him, realisation dawning on her face. He hadn't stolen her idea after all. 'I needed to find out what you knew and exactly how your device worked. I told myself that I could simply go back to Hobart, grant you an appointment and sort it out then. But, after seeing how much pressure you were under with your work and as I did have a few weeks holiday owing, I decided to stay.

'It was a mistake because only a few days later I found myself falling for you. You're the most desirable woman who's ever been able to really stir the fires within me. When you confessed your love for me I was utterly disgusted with myself for gaining your love under such false pretences.' He reached for her other hand and looked lovingly into her eyes.

'Sarah, I do return your love and want us to be together for the rest of our lives.'

'Oh, Ren.' Sarah jumped to her feet, almost overturning the entire table. He guided her around to him and sat her on his knee. His lips met hers with a pent-up passion—all inhibitions disappearing as they savoured one another.

'This is definitely not the place,' he smiled at her when they broke apart.

'Well, where *is* the place and why aren't we there?' Sarah whispered in his ear, then gasped as another thought occurred to her.

'Ren, I can't leave my home—my practice. I couldn't possibly give it all up to come back to Hobart.'

He looked at her with love in his eyes. 'I've already thought of that. I've applied to do more research and have received a grant. Full-time research, Sarah—for at least the next two years.'

'But what about your professorship?'

'I'll still lecture during that time and take leave from the hospital. When the two years are up I can always commute to Hobart, especially if Trevor teaches me how to fly!'

Sarah smothered his face with kisses. 'I love you, Ren. Please. . .can't we leave here?'

'Not yet, you little minx. Are you going to let me finish my story?'

'Maybe,' she replied, nibbling at his earlobe. Ren groaned and set her on her feet.

'Go and sit down. I can't concentrate when you're so near.' She did as he asked but continued to hold his hands. Now that she had him she was *never* going to let him go.

'Back to my story. When I found out your reasons for creating your prototype I was deeply ashamed. Your desire came out of a need in a third-world country while I merely saw a gap in the market that could be filled.'

'I don't really care about the device, Ren. You were there first so you deserve the recognition. I'm not an orthopod nor do I want to be known as an inventor. It was just an idea that seemed worth the long shot. It didn't pay off. . .end of story. Now can we go somewhere else?'

'Sarah! If you interrupt one more time I'll put you over my knee.'

'Ooh, promises. . .promises,' she teased, and Ren grinned back at her.

'I needed to borrow your prototype because the more I looked at your design the more I realised that your device had one main function that mine did not. I put it through exactly the same tests as mine, as well as some different ones, and discovered a remarkable fact. Your device is more. . .portable than mine. To clarify that, your device could be used not only in an operating theatre but also out in the field. . .in war-torn countries, third-world countries. Mine can't.' His eyes seemed filled with excitement.

'We can modify that extra part of yours and make it an attachment of mine. The FDA would never approve your device because mine is already on the market but this attachment would mean that all our hard work wasn't in vain. What do you say, Sarah? Shall we merge?'

'It depends.' She ran her tongue provocatively around her lips. 'How exactly are we merging?'

'You're continually surprising me today, Sarah Rutherford, but you do have a point.' She watched as his Adam's apple convulsed a few times. 'Is it hot in here?' He grinned. 'Do you want the entire process?'

'You bet.'

'OK. You asked for it.' He stood up and cleared his throat. 'May I have your attention, please?' He faced the café full of people and suddenly everyone was quiet. 'I'm afraid that I need your assistance for a few moments as I would like several people to witness the

momentous event that is about to take place.' He turned
back to Sarah, walked over to stand beside her then
bent on one knee. Taking her hand in his, he looked
into her now-startled and slightly embarrassed face.

'Sarah Jane Rutherford, I love you with all my heart.
Will you do me the honour of becoming my wife?'

Sarah looked around at the sea of faces which were
all grinning at her. . .strangers, waiting eagerly to hear
her reply. She focused her attention back to Ren and
giggled.

'I'd be delighted.'

A cheer went up and everyone clapped as they sealed
their declarations with a passion-searing kiss.

'I'll get you for this,' Sarah whispered into his ear.

'I can't wait.'

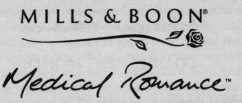

MILLS & BOON®

Medical Romance™

*Don't miss Josie Metcalfe's wonderfully
heartwarming trilogy...*

St Augustine's Hospital

*We know you'll love getting to know
this fascinating group of friends*

FIRST THINGS FIRST
Nick and Polly's story
in October

SECOND CHANCE
Wolff and Laura's story
in November

THIRD TIME LUCKY
Leo and Hannah's story
in January

St Augustine's: where love surprises everyone

MILLS & BOON®

Medical Romance™

COMING NEXT MONTH

INCURABLY ISABELLE by Lilian Darcy

Isabelle returns to her roots in France, determined to heal a long-standing family rift, but, made apprehensive by a friend, she keeps her identity secret from her second cousin, Jacques—a mistake, when they fell in love.

HEART OF GOLD by Jessica Matthews
Sisters at Heart

Kirsten is committed to her clinic helping the poor, but its future is uncertain. She reluctantly accepts the help of Jake, unaware he is responsible for the uncertainty.

FIRST THINGS FIRST by Josie Metcalfe
St Augustine's

Nick can't face the anniversary of his wife's death; Polly won't let him give in, but when did comforting turn into love?

WINGS OF LOVE by Meredith Webber
Flying Doctors—final episode

Base Manager Leonie had survived one bad marriage—loving Alex was a risk, one she might not take, particularly if it meant living in Italy!

Meet
A PERFECT FAMILY

Shocking revelations and heartache lie just beneath the surface of their charmed lives.

The Crightons are a family in conflict. Long-held resentments and jealousies are reawakened when three generations gather for a special celebration.

One revelation leads to another - a secret war-time liaison, a carefully concealed embezzlement scam, the illicit seduction of another's wife. The façade begins to crack, revealing a family far from perfect, underneath.

"Women everywhere will find pieces of themselves in Jordan's characters"
–Publishers Weekly

The coupon is valid only in the UK and Eire against purchases made in retail outlets and not in conjunction with any Reader Service or other offer.

50p OFF
COUPON
VALID UNTIL: 31.12.1997

PENNY JORDAN'S *A PERFECT FAMILY*

9 904170 210508

0472 00195